Pretty little mess

A Jane Luck Adventure

By Joy Outlaw

Pretty Little Mess: A Jane Luck Adventure

OmniMind Media

Cover Graphics by
Melissa Wales

ISBN 978-0-9971827-0-5 (Print)
ISBN 978-0-9971827-1-2 (eBook)

Join the Adventure

There's more to come from the Jane Luck Adventures series and from Joy Outlaw. Stay in the know about new book releases, events, and giveaways, and join intriguing chats with the author and other readers.

Get Joy's next book and post your amazon reviews here:
amazon.com/author/joyoutlaw

Follow Joy here:
www.inanna-joy.com
Instagram @inannajoy
Facebook facebook.com/inanna.joy.1

Acknowledgements

My sincerest "Thank you" goes out to:

My family for riding the waves with me.

My village for the laughs, prayers, positive intentions, and advice.

My mentor for patiently guiding me through my journey.

My friends for being there, and for never letting me partake of a bottle of Patron alone when the you-know-what hits the fan.

Life's gifts and teachers, the entire cast and crew without whom there would be no story and not nearly enough color.

Dedication

To you... yeah, YOU.

Grab your favorite drink and enjoy!

Part 1

The heart has its own mind.

1

I know I'm not a weak person, but everybody has a breaking point.

"Just step back and take a break, honey." she said. "There is nothing wrong with taking it slow. You don't want to have a nervous breakdown."

My mom was on a rant, but she was at least partly right. I could feel myself straddling a cliff emotionally, and I wanted to avoid the dreaded breakdown that could take me out if I wasn't careful.

My mom went on.

"You know, I really think that's what happened to your aunt Gloria. She used to be alright. She went out, interacted with people. She used to babysit you and Terence when you were little. Then she started that talking to herself. I really think her husband's overdose and losing that job sent her over the edge. Does she still sit in the dark dining room with her arms folded after everybody else is done eating holiday dinner at your Grandma Celia's?"

"Sometimes." I said. "She seems a little better since she started getting out more to volunteer at that church, though. That's good to see."

"And what about your uncle Jean? Does he talk at all anymore?"

"Well, you know he pretty much avoids contact. But if we're at Granny's house at night, he comes out of his room like clockwork for something to eat. He'll mumble hello when he passes the living room, but that's pretty much it."

"Huh." mom sighed. "It's such a shame that y'all didn't really get a chance to know them. And Jean was so talented."

"I know, I think about that every time I see them or one of his paintings lying around the house."

"Keep praying, honey. That's all you can do."

Gloria and Jean were my father's siblings, apparently products of the same traumas that fueled my dad's drug addiction. Their family history along with my mother's own past experience with depression and suicidal thoughts caused her to be very concerned for my well-being whenever I started stressing school.

"I'ma tell you like I told you when you were in high school and trying to take all those advanced classes. Life is too short to be stressing yourself out. You do not have to prove anything to anybody. If this is too much, just stop and do something different."

"Yes of course, simply quit— again!" I thought, already becoming annoyed.

"I know this is your dream, but you can't be too hard on yourself. When you were sitting up all hours of the night trying to get all those papers done in that advanced

English class, PLUS, the advanced Biology work, PLUS, physics, i-it was just too much! I know you felt better when you just went back to the regular classes. Honey, you have to understand that you cannot count on man's wisdom. That alone is not gonna get you where you need to be. *'What does it profit a man to gain the whole world and lose his soul?'* Have you been praying about your classes?"

By now, my eyes had glazed over, but the phone felt like it was glued to my palm. Exasperated, I just said, "Yes."

"Have you found a church home? Ain't nothin' but the Lord that kept me from losing my mind all those years. We have to make time to advance the Kingdom. I'm telling you, in this day and age, the most important work you can do is the work of winning souls for Christ. Of course, we have to work to survive in this world and we want to use the talents God gave us… You know what I mean."

"Um hmm."

"You know I'm proud of you for making it this far. You didn't settle, and you did what you always wanted to do. We don't know what the future holds, but whatever happens, I know that you will do well because you are strong and the Lord is ordering your steps. It's just gon' take more time than it may take others to get there."

I was happy that she ended on a positive note rather than rehashing the suggestion that I consider another path. I had wanted to be an architect since I was eight years old and any other outcome, after I had already come so far, was unthinkable.

However, I had already established a bad habit of taking my parents' advice to *"just quit"* whenever I felt like I was in over my head. The consequences were in full effect. I didn't have the time management skills to shoulder sixteen credit hours in a curriculum with a reputation for turning young adults into sleepless masochists. My eye for detail was completely void of any ability to prioritize tasks, and my tendency to linger in the minutia of every assignment caused many of them to go unfinished.

The idea of taking fewer classes per semester felt like a cop-out, because I was still stuck on the fact that I had done so well in high school. I *should* have been able to do well. After all, I had been an "A" student and an honor grad.

In college, I had even studied abroad doing research partially funded by the Fulbright program and acted as an advisor to professors at my school who wanted to make Fulbright programs available to more students.

Most importantly, I was a devoted Christian in whom the Spirit of Excellence had been instilled through many altar calls and youth group conferences. Failure would be out of character, and quitting was no longer an option. The achievement of my goals would be my hard-earned reward. I wasn't asking for the journey to be easy.

While my mom spoke I remained respectful. I knew she had the best of intentions, and I chose to appreciate that fact.

"I know you only want what's best for me."

"That's right, honey. Listen, I gotta get ready to lay down and get some rest— you know I gotta work tonight. But just lemme say a lil' prayer with you before I go."

"Oh," she said as she remembered something I was kind of hoping she had forgotten.

"How's that young man you were telling me about?"

She was asking me about Jack, who was hardly a *"young man"* in the sense that she probably meant it. He was fifteen years older than me, and my interest in him had become something that would definitely inspire another lecture.

She had no idea how deep things were getting with Jack. I wondered why I had even mentioned him to her, but I was still not very far removed from that stage in my life where I was her shadow and told her everything.

My heart beat a little faster at the thought of him. Then, in a cagey manner that I rarely reserved for my mom I replied,

"He's doing well!"

We offered heartfelt and unabashedly Pentecostal-style prayers for my success, peace of mind, and the clearing of my next student loan payout. Then we went in on requests for her strength to keep pulling more than her fair share on her overnight nursing home job where the devil was busy trying to wear her out by way of some *"lazy, lyin' co-workers"*. Then we said good night.

***

"She said *WAT?!*" Celine screamed in a high-pitched accent seasoned with the essence of Jamaican Patois.

I sighed and paused before putting a spoonful of fruit salad in my mouth.

"She said, *'I'm glad the Lord saved you when he did, because I thought you were gon' turn out to be a lil' ho.'* "

Celine shook her head and blinked her eyes as if fighting off a sudden blast of wind. She then repeated,

"… *WAT?!!*"

"I could NOT say anything else after that. She was talking about how proud she was of me and how my future could have been derailed if I had a boy crazy phase in my teens like so many other girls. I think I'm gonna have to put my big girl drawers on and keep the Jack thing to myself."

"Why would she think that?"

Celine's demand for an understanding of all this was echoed in the banging of her spoon against her plate as she spoke.

"I've always been outgoing, kind of curious, liked to be on the go. My personality is a lot like my dad's. I think she saw that and automatically jumped to the conclusion that I'd take on his negative habits, too. You remember how she went on that fast when she saw me having a glass of champagne in my study abroad video."

"Of *all* the positive conclusions she could get from outgoing and curious she settled on *whore*?"

"It's such a long story." I said with a deadpan stare.

I stepped over to a nearby trashcan to clear my tray then went back to the table to load up my stuff. After putting on my coat, I put on my full backpack, then the large 3'x3' fabric tote which held my art class assignments. I put the brand new roll of tracing paper under my arm, grabbed the plastic tackle box which housed my drawing tools with one hand, and took my foam core architectural concept model with the other.

Celine was the least bogged down of us. She only had a large purse and her own tackle box full of sewing tools and fabric scraps. She held the door for me as we left the dining hall.

"Dammit, it's supposed to snow again tonight." she said.

She was as sure-footed as a mountain goat, stepping lightly over icy patches of sidewalk while clutching her faux-fur-trimmed coat. Her devotion to fashion was justified only by the fact that fashion design was her field of study. She was no slave it, though. Celine refused to spend more than ten bucks for *any* single item and was always up for a thrift store scavenger hunt. I had given up my obsession with cute clothes and stilettos many broke and sleep-deprived moons ago.

I took a good look at the white night sky above and said,

"You know, I'm actually starting to get used to this weather. I'm embracing the changing seasons and the sharp differences in temperature. Plus having my new place helps. There's nothing like turning out the lights, cranking up the heat, yanking off all my clothes, and staring out the picture windows with a cup of hot tea in my hands."

"Using part of that financial aid money for off campus housing was a good move." Celine said.

"Yep!" I agreed. "And finding something so nice for $650 a month was amazing. But I almost didn't get the apartment."

"Really?"

"No credit or cosigner. So I just offered to pay the first six months up front. Money talks. A year in my apartment actually costs less than on campus housing, and it's *so* much better!"

"Hey, speaking of that," Celine said, "...I was thinking..."

Her speech slowed for the first time that evening as she said *"thin-king"*, and I could feel a really big thought coming.

"This RA thing is takin' up too much of my time and these kids are nuts!"

Her speech was back at top speed.

"Last night, I was tryin' to finish a garment for review and some *fool* ran down the hall drunk and threw up all over the carpet! After I wrote him up for *scribblin'* all over the walls with magic marker, his dad calls me and proceeds to cuss me out!"

While she ranted, I stared upward as if trying to read whatever she had scribbled into the air in a fit of hand gesturing.

She continued, "Cussed me out! Talking 'bout, *'Who do you think you are? My son's tuition, room, and board are paid in full! He's no scholarship kid! Let him have some fun!'* "

I could feel her skinny index finger through my coat as she poked at my chest for emphasis.

"Can you believe that?!"

"See, that's the same mess I couldn't wait to get away from." I said. "My place is awesome. No loud, 3am music, messy roommates, or privileged snots with Fetal Entitlement Syndrome in sight. There's just this weird old guy downstairs who complains about noise coming from my place at times when I'm not even at home. But I think he may just be a little senile or something."

Celine stopped walking and looked at me like a child about to ask for a new bike for Christmas.

"Well…maybe *one* messy roommate?"

I looked away from her and stared off into the distance with a smirk. I knew what she wanted before she asked, and she probably already knew that the answer was yes.

"You know there is almost *no* on campus housing available for upperclassman, and I really need more time to focus next semester. This Resident Assistant job gets me free housing, but it's really not free since I have to put so much time and energy into dealing with this craziness. I can't afford to live off campus on my own."

She turned to me again.

"And I can't really afford to live off campus with a roommate either. My scholarship can only be applied to classes."

Then the begging started.

"So *pleeeease,* can I spend next semester with you?"

Groveling was totally unnecessary, but that did not stop her from sacrificing her zebra print jeans (which she got on super discount at Off 5th) as she kneeled by the roadside to show her contrition.

"I will cook, I'll clean, I won't be messy, I'll take out the trash! You won't have to do anyth—"

"Please, girl!"

Passersby were starting to give us crazy looks!

"You know I don't mind. But what are you gonna do for the summer and next year?"

"Oh, Leslie and I are planning to get a place together once the Summer rolls around and we can work more hours at our jobs. Some guy she knows from the mail room hooked us up, so we talked to management at this apartment complex near Schoolhouse and Wissahickon. He's gonna give us a good price on a unit that will be vacant then."

"Okay, well… if there's anybody I don't mind living with, it's you. I know you'll respect my place. But just one thing— you know my place is my den. I like to be *comfortable* in my den."

Celine was well aware of the fact that I had developed a habit of not wearing clothes at home. I guess it was an extended expression of my newfound liberty, and I wasn't going to clip my own wings for anybody.

"Oh hell, I don't care about that." she laughed. "What you got that I ain't seen? As long as I don't have to keep seeing a bunch of passed out drunks with nasty rolls hanging out of their shirts and running mascara, rock on, sista!"

"Plus… I might be spending some time away. A house sitter will be a good thing." We both stopped laughing.

"Where are *you* goin'?" Celine asked.

Though I knew our friendship was one forged in respect and understanding, from time to time I still got the sense that Celine thought she had me figured out. And I hated it when anybody assumed they had me figured out. It was like being boxed up, labeled and shipped off, never to be seen again.

Leslie was Celine's fun friend, the one she went out dancing with and the one she indulged in the occasional excursion to the Wave (the local strip joint for chicks) with. They were both twenty-one, pursuing the same major, and were like two peas in a pod.

I was the older friend— only twenty-four, but I might as well had been thirty. I was the serious (sometimes too serious) one who sometimes gave her advice when she was overwhelmed, the one who she could catch a ride to church with on Sunday morning, and the one who'd let her crash for a semester rent-free. I wasn't expected to have much of a life.

"I haven't decided yet. I-I don't even know for sure if I'm going away yet, but I've been thinking about it. Maybe it'll just be for a week or something… after exams. I don't know."

"You'll be fine." She reassured me with sincerity. "You, of all people, will be fine."

2

Where did Jack find these guys? I'm sure he was just keeping his expenses and paperwork low. That was the only reason I could think of for why he would take on some of the characters he hired to monitor his investment properties. And he had this thing about trying to give jobs to younger people from the neighborhood who might not otherwise have these kinds of opportunities.

This dude looked like Lurch from *The Addams Family.* He was rocking a Gumby-ish hairstyle that was uncombed (presumably for days) and in need of a serious shape up.

I sat outside on the North Philly stoop for nearly ten minutes watching Temple students rush by before he finally opened the door and slid halfway through it while glaring across the street. If he hadn't opened the door for me, I would have thought he didn't even see me.

I stood up, but I wasn't about to go in.

"You can come up." he said with a groggy voice.

"You know where Jack is?" I asked.

"Center City, gettin' paperwork. He be here in like twenty minutes."

"I'll wait."

His eyes opened fully, for the first time, with a hint of surprise as he processed my refusal to enter a boarded up house with him. Some nerve! I sat back down on the stoop and waited another seven minutes for Jack.

When he arrived, I wanted to kick myself for being caught off guard, again. My poker face didn't show it, but it always took me a few seconds to recover from being thrown off my emotional center when he looked at me and smiled. Looking into his eyes was like looking into the sun— if I stared I'd be blinded by his good looks and by the fear that he didn't see something just as beautiful when he looked at me.

One of my professors introduced me to Jack about a month earlier. This professor had also advised a couple of meetings of the Alliance of Minority Students in Design, of which I was a member. He understood that mentorship and community involvement was important to me, and he told me that he knew a guy who was a real estate investor and had interest in being a developer.

He described the guy as *"probably one of the few people interested in preserving some of the current community dynamic"*. This meant that while so much redevelopment in the neighborhoods in Philly had included getting rid of the poor and minorities, this guy's idea of improvement didn't necessarily involve such displacement. I wanted to meet him right away, because I wanted to talk to him and find out how he planned to get things done.

I was relieved that he wasn't like some of the blacks I'd met in the academic world since transferring to the small, private Fairmont University. He was unpretentious and welcoming. His introduction wasn't riddled with questions meant to determine my level of societal grooming, how much money I came from, or what prestigious organizations I had or had not been granted access to. He wasn't like some of the African and Caribbean immigrants who seemed to go out of their way in being aloof toward other blacks. Those types didn't want to appear partial and would tell us to our faces that they were "not black" in an effort to separate themselves from the African American stereotype.

Jack was clearly competent, comfortable in his own skin and with his humble roots. The fact that he was fine and so friendly that he acted like he already knew me when we were introduced was icing on the cake.

He got out of his car and glanced at the ground while he stepped carefully onto the sidewalk. This gave me a few seconds to get a good look at his runner's frame.

He wasn't one of those sick-looking runners, either. He was into functional fitness training and recreational boxing, so he was as toned and strong as he was trim. Not bad at all for thirty-nine.

He looked up and saw me sitting on the stoop. As he wrapped up a phone conversation he threw his hands up as if to say, *"What gives?"* I pointed toward the door and shook my head. He gave me a sympathetic squeeze on the shoulder before knocking on the door.

"No, I'm sorry, I don't agree. The bank may be able to offer you lower interest and a shorter term, but they will not cover your rehab costs. You'll be required to have an inspection done before financing can occur and you won't be able to double close, so any deals you're considering with a wholesaler are out. Plus, you're looking at a possible 30-60 day close with a bank. I can help you get it done in 10."

I could tell he was becoming irritated with whoever was on the phone. He looked at me and shook his head.

"Yes, cash would be the best way to go, but that means you could only afford to do one deal rather than the three you're considering, right? Long run means less money down, higher return on investment. More deals, more equity, more income."

He pulled the phone away from his face and quietly said, "You should know that." Then he flashed a plastic smile to force himself to continue sounding upbeat despite his annoyance— a trick he told me he learned working at a bank call center.

"Exactly… tomorrow at 3. That works for me. See you then."

He knocked on the door one more time before shoving his phone into his pocket. His demeanor immediately switched from business to much more casual.

"Man, where the hell is this fool?!"

"He was just in there a while ago." I said.

"Why he ain't let you in?"

"Felt safer out here."

He looked at the door and squinted his eyes like he was trying to figure out what I meant.

"He was acting funny, huh? I shoulda sent Judy over here today, but she couldn't get a babysitter. Sorry 'bout that. This boy has some issues lately, but when I need him to open up a property so somebody else can see it he's normally alright."

I stumbled internally again— just a little— when Jack motioned to unlock the door. We were almost huddling to avoid the wind, and a bewitching cloud of Tom Ford Black

Orchid floated out from underneath his wool jacket and plaid scarf.

I was noting the lovely contrast that his jet black beard created against his like-new skin, which was just a shade lighter than mine. India Arie's *Brown Skin* began playing inside my head, but I snapped out of it when he looked at me again. He was taller than me, but not so much that he needed to lean very far when he spoke into my ear.

"It's too cold for this. You should lemme take you for coffee later to make up for it."

Just then the door jerked open and Lurch came flying out with his coat halfway on. Before he could barrel down the stairs and onto that street he couldn't keep his eyes off of, Jack grabbed him by the collar and reminded him,

"Keys!"

Lurch handed him the keys. Jack put them in his pocket and quietly watched Lurch step into the street again before asking, "You want your money or what?"

Lurch stopped quickly and bent over a little to brace himself as he turned back around.

"I thought you was gonna pay me on the regular day."

Jack gave him a long, questioning look in the eyes then took fifty bucks out of his pocket. I could see that Lurch was just as thrown off by Jack's steamy gaze as I always was, but not for the same reason.

When he reached for the money, Jack pulled back and said, "I'm taking twenty back. That's penalty for your presentation."

Lurch sighed and shook his head, but he took the money and turned back toward the street.

"I won't be using him again. I ain't even wanna wait to pay him. See, this is why I need your help." Jack held the door open for me.

"I wouldn't have to take on these random day workers if I had somebody like you to check on the properties. I'm sick of taking all these calls. Plus you need to start spending some time around the contractors so you can get used to their kind. Them professors got y'all kids clueless."

Jack had a point, but I knew bait when I saw it. Offering me a chance to be his mentee was his way of securing a long-term business and romantic partner. It was obvious from day one that he was attracted to me, too. From the incessant offers of coffee to a few well-timed text invitations to some concert or the movies, his flirting game was all the way on.

"I'm 'bout to wholesale a few more properties in Fishtown and I could really use somebody to take these phone calls, help me with the property assessments, talk to the buyers. I got people, but I can't trust anybody enough to show them the ropes like that."

"Uh, I dunno." I said. "Those calls and requests for viewings come in all day, and I can't be traveling between here and campus all the time like that. The hours would be too irregular."

"Well, I mean, I don't expect you to be running back and forth like that. I'm just saying, if you could block out a few hours in the day to check messages, show a property— like one per day on a weekly schedule— get a little paperwork done… get a bite to eat, my treat…"

"Vacant houses aren't the safest place for me to be frequenting." I said, keeping the conversation on target.

He sucked his teeth. "Don't nobody mess with my shit."

He gave me that deadly undereyed look and waited for me to take him at his word.

"The houses, I mean. And you wouldn't have to keep driving around with that situation if you took that car I offered you."

He was talking about the ashy, matte black section that had replaced the driver side fender on my otherwise golden Chevy Cavalier. It had been hit by a drunk driver while parked on the street outside my apartment. Since I only had liability insurance and the person who hit my car had none, I was only able to have it repaired enough to make the car functional again.

Even so, his offer of a car was hardly tempting. Seemed like he still hadn't figured out that I wasn't so easily moved by the prospect of material things. Plenty of guys were just as abundantly idiotic as they were abundantly wealthy.

I was, however, impressed by his grit, by the fact that he had achieved significant professional and financial progress as a result of many years of perseverance. He came from my side of the tracks, and I could learn a lot from him.

"I'd rather take it one project at a time." I said. "The drawings first."

He gave up, for the time being, and said, "Alright." Then he flipped on a spotlight in a corner of the would-be living room.

"You were all clean cut on that call." I said. "I've never heard you go into total pro mode with investors you already know."

"He's a newbie, at least when it comes to financing. Academic type, another professor. I had to remove what could be a... perception barrier."

"Oh, really?" I said.

I took out my sketchbook and tape measure and started recording dimensions for the remodel drawings that he'd hired me to complete.

"We inhabit many worlds, Jane. You have to choose the mode of communication which fits the circumstance."

"Oh, I know all about that." I said.

Jack continued, "Like this situation; I ain't gotta be in pro mode with you, because this situation… is not professional."

"It isn't?" I asked, feigning surprise.

His expression revealed an equal sense of shock at my response, and he turned away with a laugh as I sketched.

Jack made some phone calls and went around checking the windows and plumbing to make sure nothing had been tampered with.

By the time I made it to the upstairs bathroom he was done, and I turned around to find him standing in the doorway casually staring at me— okay, probably more like assmiring me.

"Yes?" I asked.

"Is that a question or a reply?"

"Why would it be a reply when you haven't asked me anything?"

"Oh, okay." He lingered for a few more seconds as I continued sketching a reconfiguration of the bath and shower combo.

"Alright, young buck." he said, finally. "I'll leave you alone and let you work."

"Thank you."

3

Another quiz barely passed. I didn't even look it over. I was exhausted and just happy to be going home for the day.

The sad part was that I was fascinated by physics. When I actually had the time to read the text and understand the real world applications, the math was much easier to figure out. But my mind was not nearly as quick as it needed to be to make anything more than a borderline failing grade in Structures, which was basically physics for buildings. I always finished a semester in the Structures series wondering how I would ever figure out how to actually make a building stand.

I had no idea how I'd pass the upcoming exam, so I just said a prayer and stopped caring.

I stopped by the studio to grab some supplies from my desk and ran into my Design instructor, Professor Cheyney, on the way out.

"Jane, can I talk to you for a few minutes?"

"What is it now?" I thought. *"I figured I was doing okay on the Living Memorial project."*

Prof. Cheyney gestured for me to follow her as she walked down the hall.

"Come over to my office. It won't take too long."

I felt surprisingly comfortable in her office. She kept the lamp off in favor of the natural light from a large window. Everything was neat, and the top of her desk was organized with a sleek, stainless steel clock, a few drafting pencils in a matching cup, and the tracing paper that she had used for demonstrations in class that morning. Her Restoration Hardware-style, French Panel Cabinet was packed with neatly stacked books on architectural theory and history.

I liked her style. I was never the kind of student to spend much time schmoozing with professors, but I didn't mind visiting her for the first time.

She slowly eased into her seat across from me. It was like she was trying to tread lightly, like she didn't know how I would respond to what she was going to share. Maybe she was just trying to feel me out.

I'd had a few talks with other professors who seemed almost afraid to approach me before asking me if there was anything they could do to help me improve my performance. They had looked into my eyes as if searching for some assurance that I wouldn't become volatile upon hearing whatever they had to say.

Prof. Cheyney was different. Rather than fear, she seemed to exude a sense of understanding. At least she was *trying* to understand me. She didn't pity me, because she wasn't giving me that puppy dog stare. I got a sense of something resembling respect when she leaned forward to say,

"Sometimes you can tell when a student has a unique story. It shows on her face, and it makes her a lot more insightful than the average student. As you can see, most people aren't excited about designing a cemetery, but you've been full of ideas and your conceptual models have been very alluring. You've embraced this project. Why?"

"Well, I guess it's because I see death as another form of life. It doesn't scare me… It represents ultimate peace. And memorials aren't for the dead, really, they're for the living."

I could tell that she was enjoying my perspective so I said a little more. I didn't mind letting my interest shine through a little and took the risk of waxing sentimental.

"It's a welcoming and thoughtful space where the living can make peace with their memories and feelings. It's a reminder of the beauty of life."

She paused for several moments to take in what I said.

"I get the sense that your perspective is advanced, but your skills have just not yet caught up."

"Yeah, it's a challenge keeping up and I don't have as much time to practice. CAD is giving me a hard time. I'm not really tech-inclined."

"I think you have a unique perspective to offer this profession, and it is sorely needed. I'm looking forward to seeing your final presentation." She gave me a warm smile and shook my hand as I stood to leave.

"Thank you. I appreciate the talk." I said.

"Um hmm." she responded with a nod.

***

I really did need to work on my Computer Aided Drafting skills. With everything else on my plate, I wasn't finding time to sit in the computer lab for hours and just *"play around with CAD"*. This was the suggestion that everybody gave on how to become proficient: *"Just sit for a while and play around with it."*

The computer I owned was the first I'd ever had, and I wasn't very fond of the idea of spending so much time in the unfamiliar, easily frustrating virtual world. Maybe the suggestion to *"play"* was itself throwing me off. It seemed unimportant, unnecessary, unwise even, to spend so much time playing. I figured I should be able to learn this within the confines of instruction. I never even considered the possibility that enjoying it could actually help me learn it.

I also didn't know which one of my classmates to ask for their pirated copy of the several-thousand-dollar CAD program they used for assignments. Even if I was cool enough with any of them to ask for the hook up, I didn't have the funds to purchase the additional memory my computer needed to run it.

My only option would be to camp out in the computer lab several times a week whenever it wasn't already packed, or whenever I didn't have more pressing assignments… or whenever I didn't have to go to work… or whenever I wasn't in an antisocial, lights out and sound off kind of mood.

3-D modeling was my real area of deficiency, but I could do floorplans easily enough. So before going home, I decided to work on Jack's drawings. It was a Thursday evening. A lot of kids were getting ready to go out, so there weren't many people in the lab. I put on my headphones, cranked up Radio Mystery Theater on

Live365, and completed the drawings two weeks before I had initially planned.

I got home, took a long bubble bath, and gave Jack a call.

"You done already?" he asked, surprised and happy.

"Yep. When do you want them?"

"I can pick them up tomorrow."

"I'll be in Center City doing some research for class tomorrow. I don't mind bringing them by."

"I can save you some time and pick them up now."

Silence on my end. Eye roll.

"You still don't want me coming to your place." he said.

"That's not a problem, I'm just trying to make things easier for you." I said.

"No you're not… Okay, so how 'bout I take you to breakfast tomorrow morning, you give me the drawings, and I pay you. In that order. It's a business breakfast. I wanna get your opinion on some potential investments I'm looking at."

I thought about it and figured an opportunity to learn more about Jack's business was a good one.

"Yeah… okay." I said.

***

When Jack saw the drawings at breakfast the next morning he was as relieved as I was to have them done.

"Man, you don't know how glad I'ma be to get rid of this house."

"You're gonna sell it?"

"Yeah!"

"I thought you might hold on to it and rent it out."

"Not to no college kids— no offense."

"None taken."

"Nah, I'm flipping this one. There's a block of houses I'm looking at in West Philly that I'm interested in turning into a co-op. That's where I'm investing the money from the wholesaling and flips. And I'm not into that low-income housing shit. I'm tryna get outta the landlord business."

"So a co-op isn't affordable?"

"No, a co-op can be very affordable. But what you don't spend in money, you have to make up for in community involvement. You can't just live there, hole up in your lil' corner, and not care about what goes on in the neighborhood. That's ownership on another level. And it's not like having some homeowner's association nitpicking about paint colors. It's self-government."

This was the reason I had wanted to study architecture all these years. I wanted to make an impact by creating beautiful living spaces that would bring out the best in individuals and communities. As a black woman in the profession, I also wanted to see the effects of good design along with transgenerational wealth at work in the kinds of communities that I was used to living in.

Now that I'd had a chance to experience what my profession was really about, it seemed like the kind of work Jack did could get me closer to that goal.

After he finished telling me all about bandit signs and yellow postcards, free voicemail services and cashflow properties, I almost felt like I could start an ad campaign to wholesale some houses myself.

"So you guys are the ones posting all those *We Buy Houses* signs all over the place." I said.

"Yeah, you thought it was a bunch of white boys trying to buy up the neighborhood and pay grandma and grandpop pennies for it."

"Pretty much."

"Hey, I ain't mad about redevelopment, or gentrification— whatever you wanna call it. I'm just disappointed in us for not redeveloping some of that property ourselves. Why can't *we* be the gents? Can't blame them for buying it if it's for sale."

"Yeah, but we've tried that, right? Black Wall Street, Rosewood, those black business corridors and co-ops like the ones the Muslims created— you know what happens. Where are they now?"

"Some of them are still out there, they're just low key. You gotta stop internalizing those pitiful black folk statistics, Jane. Numbers lie, okay, it just depends on who tallied them and why. Yeah, we got problems, but while a lot of us are sitting around shaking our heads at the news, just talking and wringing our hands over the supposed dire state of black America, some of us are getting shit done."

He had a point.

"You *could* start wholesaling. Now would be the time to do it, and you don't need any kind of license for it. Some of the guys I know bought their first houses in their early twenties. While you spending time taking classes, they're flipping properties. That's a trip, right? School ain't a bad idea, though. I just met a guy who's using his student loans to rehab a property not too far from here... Of course, I'm not trying to be your competition."

"Look, Jack," I said, determined to put an end to his effort to reel me in. "I really appreciate you giving me the opportunity to work with you and all the things you've shared with me, but now is just not a good time. I really need to focus on making the most of my study time."

"Yeah, but you still need to *work*."

"And I have two other jobs."

"Does the graduate admissions office or the museum pay you $1000 a week? How 'bout doing hair, how much you making off that hustle?"

I ignored his comments and considered how much I'd eventually have to pay *him* if he really became a fixture in my life.

"How 'bout that club you're in— have any of those *professionals* that you contacted for mentorship called y'all back yet?"

I hadn't told him about that.

"How do you know about AMSD?"

"Your professor said something about it. And I bet they ain't got not one black nobody featured in that career development series they're getting ready to have."

He chomped casually on his pancakes while doing all he could to piece apart my little plan for advancement, then wrapped up his appeal.

"Well, look, if you need more time to think about it and make room for the opportunity, I understand. The offer's on the table."

He seemed upset, but I guess he was willing to let it go in favor of a pleasant end to our meal.

***

There is nothing like leaving the studio after a draining critique, knowing that the semester is over, and going home to rest after a week of three-hour-a-night power sleeping.

After intriguing the critic panel with my Living Memorial presentation, I was glad to walk away with some encouraging words and an intact ego.

Students in neighboring corners of the studio weren't so lucky. When everyone flooded out of the building after crits, a few of them could be seen smashing their models against walls, wiping away tears as they talked to friends, or cursing at the top of their lungs.

I reached into my purse after feeling a pulse indicating a text message.

Jack: *"How'd it go?"*

Had I told Jack when my crit would be? I must have mentioned it at some point.

Since that last time we met in person, he had messaged me regularly just to check on me. He had not only taken a romantic interest in me, he also seemed concerned about my career and my well-being.

Jane: *"Didn't get cursed out or have my model dismantled before my eyes. Good all around. I think the wine kept the professors relaxed."*

Jack: *"Congrats on another semester."*

I took off my hood and let some scattered snowflakes fall on my face before getting into my car. The crisp air was refreshing, but also a reminder that my cozy apartment and a generous portion of Rum Cream were waiting for me.

I threw everything into the back seat and adjusted the radio to Smooth Jazz 106.1. Then another text came through.

Jack: *"How about a concert to celebrate?"*

Jane: *"When?"*

Jack: *"This weekend."*

Jane: *"Who?"*

Jack: *"A keeper of the soul flame you might like."*

Jane: *"…Why not?"*

Jack: *"…Exactly."*

It was time to stop giving the guy such a hard time and to let myself have a good time. I couldn't blame him for being sincere or persistent, and I did feel a little bad for upsetting him at breakfast. Working for him may not be a good idea, but a concert couldn't hurt.

4

"Rashida's on cornbread and chocolate cake." Jessica said.

"Oh my god, Rashida's cornbread with the little pieces of corn in it and baked in a skillet?" I asked. "Sho nuff!"

"Celine is doing cabbage and potatoes."

"I don't have time to do no more than that!" Celine chimed in from across the room in Jessica's apartment.

"I'm doing curry chicken, cucumber salad, and rice and beans. And Jane, you've got pot roast and collard greens."

"And corn on the cob." I added.

"Don't wanna miss that!" Jessica double checked her list then said, "We're gonna have to *charge* these guys to come in and eat all this food that they won't be cooking."

"Put 'em on dish duty." I said with an affirmative nod.

"Why aren't they doing the grocery shopping?" Celine asked.

"They got no car, but let's see if a pack of brainy athletes can't show themselves useful and carry some groceries on the bus."

We all started laughing while Jessica picked up her phone to call one of the guys.

We had decided to have a small dinner party that weekend before holiday break and invited our friends, soccer players Ryan, Irving, and Shawn. Being among the handful of Black students on campus, we shared common perspectives and hung kind of tight. The blend of cultures that each of us brought to the mix made for a lot of interesting conversation and amazing meals.

Jessica was pre-med. She was from Trinidad, as were Ryan and Irving who both majored in business. Shawn was from Connecticut and also studying architecture. He and I had a couple of classes together.

Rashida, along with two other friends, Anodiwa and Giselle were second generation Nigerian, South African, and Ethiopian immigrants, all studying fashion merchandising. Since Anodiwa and Giselle weren't into cooking, they'd be bringing the drinks.

"You can *bring* the dishes, or you gonna *wash* the dishes." Jessica was already starting to get heated with Irving on the phone.

"...What is so hard about what I'm saying, Irving... DIS-POS-ABLE DI-SHES."

I could hear Irving getting just as heated on the other end, and I knew that this never-ending locking of horns could literally go on for hours between these two. I grabbed the phone.

"Whassup, Irving? ... I know... How do the gentlemen feel about doing a little shopping?"

"Jane, I have *no* problem. We have ab-so-lute-ly *no* problem with getting things from the store, okay? I simply asked her what *kinds* of disposable dishes she would prefer. This is a holiday dinner. I would prefer not to show up with simple Styrofoam plates. We should have something sturdier, something with a little more *style*."

"I couldn't agree more, Irving." I said. "How bout y'all check out this website called smarty-had-a-party.com. See what looks good, what's reasonably priced. Expedite the shipping. It'll save you some time and an extra trip."

"That...that is wonderful. *Perfect,* Jane. That is exactly what I was after. Thank you so much."

"Thank *you*, Irving."

"Now, Jane, will you be cooking some of that splendid fried chicken that southern hosts are famous for?"

"Nuh uh. I don't fry, bruh. But I think you will be more than happy with what's on the menu."

"I am looking forward!"

I handed the phone back to Jessica and she immediately hung it up.

"She doesn't even know if he was still on there!" Celine yelled from the kitchen.

"Who cares." Jessica sang with abandon. "So, Jane... will Jack be joining us for dinner?"

I rolled my eyes while Celine decided to answer for me.

"Nope!"

"Jane! The man has to eat. This is a holiday celebration, in the spirit of our Lord Jesus."

I sat on the couch and patiently took the blows of sarcasm until I was sure Jessica had gotten it out of her system.

"Why, in God's name, would you deprive him of a meal with all your lovely friends?"

"That man ain't missing no meals. Have you seen his car?" Celine yelled. "He's been on her like white on rice and she'll barely break bread with him."

"I know." Jessica said while easing up close to me. "That's cuz he knows what's good for him. He don't want no dingbat. He's trying to put you on serious lock and key."

"And that's exactly why he can stay wherever he is Sunday and have a meal." I said.

"They're going to a concert Saturday night. He may not have the strength to come back out again Sunday."

Celine would not stop blabbing or poking fun.

Jessica's eyes widened along with her smile.

"A concert, huh? Well, Celine, let's give her a little more time to warm up to him. I'm sure after a night of *dancing* she'll be happy enough to cook an entire spread just for him."

I denied every insinuation.

"It ain't even gonna be that kind of night."

"Ooo-kay," Jessica said. "but you know Dr. Waverly's Sex Talk comes on Friday nights at ten. You may wanna watch it with us to get some pointers. You know I been takin' notes for my much anticipated first encounter. And ya betta be prepared with some protection."

Celine jumped in again, just knowing that nothing besides a shared appreciation of music would happen Saturday.

"Ah, she ain't gonna do nothing. Too much at stake."

I held out my palm in Celine's direction and nodded with a stoic grin. Then we all dropped the subject and quieted down for some reading.

5

"They got married *today*?!"

I couldn't believe what my brother Terrence was telling me.

"They did that thing to-day."

"You have got to be kidding me!"

"I wish I was, sis."

"So, because we didn't just go along with the okey doke, since we wanted her to wait and give this some more thought, we don't even get notice of the ceremony?"

"I gotta be honest with you, sis. I wouldn't have been there anyway. I can't stand the thought of him. I damn sure wouldn't be able to stand the sight of him."

"Yeah, but I told her I wanted to be there. No matter what, I wanted to be there for support. It didn't matter that I didn't agree. What kind of jerk is okay with a woman cutting her own kids out of her wedding— even though it wasn't a *wedding*?"

We both paused for a moment to decompress.

"Man, this is some mess. I gotta give her a call."

"You go ahead and call her." Terrence said. "I can't even go there right now."

When my mom picked up the phone, I tried my best to muster as much love and respect as I could. After exchanging hellos and how-do's she jumped right to the point.

"So, Jane, I don't know if you talked to Terrence or not, but Ron and I got married today."

Ron was the man my mom had met eighteen months prior. She met him through her brother-in-law who visited Virginia prisons as a minister. Ron was in the midst of serving a fifty-five year prison sentence for kidnapping and rape.

He had spent the last couple of decades as a jailhouse preacher, and when my uncle suggested she write to him, he immediately reeled her in with all the kind, romantic words she'd never heard. He suggested they get married immediately since God was apparently at work and a loving wife could look good to the parole board.

"It was a beautiful ceremony. The Chaplain was very friendly and we said our own vows that we wrote. If you want, I can share them with you."

The thought made me nauseous.

I asked, "How do you have any idea what life will be like with this man once he gets out?"

"Jane, I know it's hard for you and Terrence to understand, but God is in this thing. I know beyond a shadow of a doubt that man is saved to the bone."

"Then why doesn't he know how to exercise patience? You couldn't wait and give him a chance to prove himself? Now you're gonna sit around for a decade waiting for him to get out? You had enough horrible years with our Dad, now this? You have no idea what he'll be like once there aren't any guards around telling him what to do. Prison is all he knows!"

There was silence and I just knew that she was putting up that wall again.

"I have already told you and Terrence that I feel at peace about this, but y'all just don't want to see it. I can't believe that you could be so unforgiving. I didn't raise you like that. That man has paid his debt to society, and the only reason he's still in there is because of this racist prison system."

"Would you say that about somebody like him if I had been his victim instead of a white woman?"

She gave no answer.

"Ma, that man is near retirement age, and so are you. Who is going to provide for an extra, rusty, grown man mouth to feed? Who's gonna give him a job? He's got a violent criminal history, he's grown up in prison, and he's late middle-aged. Are you ready to spend the years that you should be resting and vacationing working extra hours instead to support the two of you?"

Once Terrence and I were grown up, I got the uncanny feeling that there had been some weird role reversal between us and our parents. It felt like we were now the guardians of two confused and naïve teens— my dad who's problems with alcohol and drugs made him unpredictable, and my mom who seemingly refused to think rationally in this situation.

"Ma, I don't mean to be disrespectful or unsupportive. We just don't want to see anybody hurt or in danger."

"I know that and I understand that. Jane, you're just going to have to trust God. Ron and I are absolutely, beyond a shadow of a doubt in love, and I know this is nothing but the Lord."

End of discussion.

***

When Jack picked me up later that night he immediately noticed that something was wrong.

"No smile again. Okay, what's up?" he asked.

"I can't talk about it right now, really. It's family stuff, really crazy family stuff."

"Alright, well I think tonight'll help you get your mind off it."

"I'm fine, really. I'm just still a little groggy from a nap I took before coming out. I'll be wide awake soon."

"You can sleep a little longer on the ride."

"Yeah, I like a good power nap, but I'm really not sleepy now."

"Even better." He pulled into a gas station and opened the door. "You'll keep me company the whole ride."

"The whole ride?"

When he got back into the car I asked, "Jack, what do you mean, *'the whole ride'*? Where is this concert?"

"Atlantic City. You didn't see the link I sent you? I emailed you the link to the ad."

Atlantic City would be over an hour-long drive from Philly. I dropped my head and tried to remember if I saw Jack's name in my inbox. I was drawing a blank. For safe measures, I sent Celine a message letting her know where we'd be.

"You didn't see the email. It's cool." He looked at me and said, "You're in good hands. All you gotta do is relax and enjoy yourself. You just hit the *Jackpot*."

I ignored his flirting with a laugh. Then a bright pair of headlights started riding his bumper the way they always do on the Schuylkill Expressway when lanes are full and someone's trying to make you go faster.

He looked into his rear view mirror and indignantly said, "Oh you can go right around me, brotha." as if the impatient driver could hear him. "Ain't gon' *make* me speed up."

I chuckled thinking of my mother who often said that very thing behind the wheel. Then I had to ask,

"Why you in a sports car driving around like Mr. Magoo?"

"Lil' girl, didn't we just leave the on-ramp? Anyway, I got precious cargo." He looked at me again and grinned.

He hit the scanner button on his radio and stopped on 900. I could tell it was AM radio by the slightly muffled sound quality.

"Who listens to AM radio?" I asked.

"What's wrong with AM radio?"

"My *grandparents* listened to talk radio. My brother and I used to fall asleep to the soothing banter of Talknet when we stayed at their house on weekends. Betta turn to something else before you nod off at the wheel!"

He shook his head and laughed. I teased him by singing the old Talknet jingle:

" 'Someone to talk to and something to share, someone you know who will always be the-e-ere… tune in, turn on, Talknet… we care!' "

"You betta stop playing wit' me. I'll have you know that this is WURD, one of the few black-owned talk radio stations in the country. I keep up with my city on this station."

"Yeah, okay." I joked.

My preference for talk radio had been WHYY, but this intrigued me. I kept that thought to myself.

He went on. "Hey, did I ever tell you about my marriages and how they ended?"

"No."

I wasn't sure why he thought I would be interested in this story, but he must have thought it would be good entertainment for the ride. It was more than entertainment, it was hilarious.

"So, I'm no spring chicken."

He was pretending to be modest, but I was sure he knew full well that his looks, charm, and intellect could overshadow any younger man's— at least to me.

"I tried the whole marriage thing a couple o' times, and man, was it a disaster. I was clueless, man. Just young and stupid. I always had a thang for feisty women and these two was crazy for real— off the chain crazy, man.

"The first one was Sheena. I used to call her Zena though, like that TV show with the warrior princess! She was light-skinned with a plump, young face and straight, dark hair with the bangs. She looked like a lil' quiet librarian, but when she was mad, she won't nothing to play with.

"Her family was from Tennessee, like out in the *country* country, in a shack in the woods somewhere. She hadn't spent too much time away from there when I met her so she wasn't all that refined. She was used to bathing outside and wringing off chicken heads, and stuff like that. I was still working at the bank then, but I had a idea to start a business, and I knew she was a hard worker and could help me out. She was game to get outta there and move to Philly."

I pictured a cross between a black version of Nell and Ma Kettle. Then I put my hand over my mouth to cover up a chuckle while he kept going.

"I wasn't always a faithful man, I'll admit that. And that's exactly how it ended. I got caught up with this chick down the street one summer and Sheena came down there cussin' me out. *'Jack whatchu think you doin' down here?! You think you gon' creep around on me?!'* "Then POP! POP-POP! Y'all woman get CRAZY, man." he said, shaking his head.

By now I couldn't hold my laughter and was bent over in my seat.

"You think that's funny?" he asked me. Even he couldn't keep from laughing.

"That's messed up! Man, that girl shot me in the left foot! I should pull over and show you the bullet wound… Nah. Anyway, I guess that was her way of stopping me from running around, so to speak. But that ain't work out too good, cuz then I met this nurse in the hospital, and that became another thang."

When he said "another thang," he leaned in and lowered his voice in that you-know-what-I-mean tone.

This was starting to sound like the inspiration for an episode of some sleazy daytime talk show. I suddenly realized that behind every seemingly polished individual probably lay *some* form of Jerry Springer-style insanity. I had no reason to feel inferior to anyone, even those seemingly more confident, wealthy, and secure kids at school.

Jack went on. "Her name was Heather. We was together for a couple of years when I messed up again. After one of her family barbecues, I started messing around with her cousin. I shoulda known that was gon' be a mess. But that girl was fast. I ain't even approach her. She was fast."

That meant she was young. I almost didn't want to know *how* young.

"Anyway, errybody called her lil' cousin 'Dink'. And they looked just alike, too. They both had the same shape and big eyes— they looked just alike. Anyway, Dink got pregnant."

He said that like he had nothing to do with it.

"A child. Okay." I thought. I let him keep going without calling him on it.

"But she ended up having a miscarriage. We was at Sonic one day getting some ice cream cones. Heather was 'sposed to be at work, but one of them mouthy girls from round the way followed my ass and told her I was at the Sonic wit Dink. Man, when she came round there I was like, *'Girl, whatchu doin here?'* And she started going off, calling the girl a ho and this, that, and the other."

I couldn't stop laughing, "She called her own cousin a ho?"

"Man, that girl was craaaa-zy! Come to find out she had a knife. Tried to slash me through the car window! Dink was scared of her, I was scared of her. I ain't know what that girl was gon' do. So I manage to get out the car to try to talk to her and keep her away from Dink. Maaan, that girl round-housed me, jumped in my car, Dink jumps out the car and runs in the Sonic. I'm thinking Dink going in there to ask for help. She goes and hides in the bathroom! I'm trying to get Heather outta my car and this chick TURNS THE CAR ON and runs over my right FOOT!"

The tears in my eyes were flowing. I didn't think I'd ever laughed so much from one story.

"She round-housed you, bruh?"

"Man, that girl was on some karate, ju-jitsu, something! I'ma show you my feet when we get to AC."

"You ain't even gotta do all that." I laughed, looking out the window with revulsion.

"Nope, I'm gon' show you, cuz you probly think I'm lyin'. This was a miracle, right here. The Lord really healed me. This my testimony."

"So what happened to Dink and Heather?" I had to know.

"Oh, they ended up moving in together after Heather mama died and left her the house. They made up, ya know. I was at least glad about that."

"Yeah, it's good to know their family stayed intact."

"I tell ya what though," Jack threw his hands up like he was in church surrendering to the Lord then quickly brought them back down to the steering wheel.

"I'm just blessed to be walking, man. That's why I can't even be living like that no mo'. I haven't really been serious 'bout nobody since then. It's just been about business and getting my stuff right. That's too much mess to be dealing with when ya get older. I'm lookin' for somebody more together, ya know, a more quiet and sensible woman. Somebody that ain't in these streets."

Though it was very faint, it sounded like I was catching on to a slight Southern accent in his voice as he spoke. But the reference to the Lord caught my attention more.

"Well, Jack, I never took you for a church-going man."

"Hey, I know how to give credit where credit is due." He put his hand over his heart and glanced at me with sincerity then continued,

"But what I hope you understand is that errybody got some kind of crazy goin' on. You know that cat I told you about that I met a few of weeks ago, that clean-cut contractor with like seventy mil in investments around North Philly and center city?"

"Yeah, the one who's kinda tight with some of the council members?"

"Man, that boy on drugs."

"Are you *serious*?"

"Straight dopehead."

"What does he do?"

"Oh, he a rich boy, so classic coke, supposedly. But somebody I know said they saw him round Tioga tryin' to cop some smack. Don't ask me how he got into that. Probly was one o' them call girls he be running with. How you let a ho turn *you* on to some dope? Anyway, I don't know how much longer he'll be functional. He got good people holdin' his business down and coverin' his tracks, so it's all good for now. See, that's why it means everything to have the right people on your team."

I nodded in agreement but said nothing more.

"So I'm hoping this crazy family stuff isn't too much of a distraction for you."

"I can't really say that it is. It adds to the layers sometimes, but, I mean, I try not to keep it in the forefront of my mind."

"Is it something ongoing or like, some new drama?"

"Both, I guess."

By now it was clear to me that Jack was someone who believed in my potential and would do whatever he could to see it realized. The fact that he hoped to benefit significantly from my development was no longer such a concern for me. That was simple give and take. He was, after all, a very savvy businessman.

I decided to tell him a little about the family issues that had been weighing on my mind, from my mother's marriage to the fist fight my dad had recently gotten into with my brother. In talking to him I realized, for the first time, that I sometimes felt guilty for leaving my big brother back home to deal with all of that. I wanted the opportunity to repay him for all his support. That was yet another reason why I couldn't give up.

As we approached the Borgota Jack said, "Yeah, that boy Seymour on that mess, too."

"Seymour?"

"That boy that was supposed to let you into one of my houses near Temple. That's why he was in such a hurry that day— tryin' to go get some testers."

"Oh, you mean Lurch?"

"Lurch?! Goddamn!" Jack laughed so hard he couldn't open his eyes. "Yeah that boy had to go… I need you on my team, Jane."

6

When we got to the Borgota, Jack stepped out of the car to speak to an approaching valet. Another whiff of his cologne hit me suddenly as the cool night air rushed into the car. Before I could recover from that, I started watching him as he buttoned up his gray peacoat.

I thought, *"How did I just make it through that ride without going catatonic?*

The valet walked briskly back into the hotel, and then returned with a bright and friendly redhead. She wasn't dressed like hotel staff but instead wore a professional, navy blue suit with a pencil skirt and burnt orange top.

"Hi, Mr. McCullough! How was the drive?"

"Not bad." Jack replied. "They salted those roads pretty well before the last ice came through."

"Good!" She stepped forward quickly to shake my hand and eyeballed the two of us as if we were about to walk down the aisle and she was sitting enthusiastically on the front row.

"And you're Jane?"

"Yes."

"Well, welcome! You two are going to have a blast here."

She flashed me a warm smile then looked back at Jack.

"Oh, I dunno how you'll make it through the evening with this one, Jane. Look at those eyes!"

Jack stood by, almost looking like he was shy.

"They're just like Billy Zane's— that guy who played Rose's jerky fiancé in *Titanic*! So dark and mysterious against that flawless skin. Ooo, you see that little twinkle! Those thick brows and the way the outer corners point just slightly downward. That hooded top lid and those flawless, youthful undereyes. I used to be a makeup artist. I would *kill* for eyes like that!"

Was this chick trying to get a good tip or what?

"And then how he looks all serious and starts blinking like that when he's thinking. Look! That is just beautiful definition. Do you wear eyeliner?"

Tip revoked.

"Uh, nah." Jack said confused, annoyed and looking toward the door.

"Well, anyway, everything's ready and absolutely flawless. You're in the Water Club tonight and—"

She caught another glance from Jack which let her know that she should finally quit talking.

"Okay. Well, enjoy yourselves and call if you need anything."

As she turned to walk away I asked Jack,

"Just a concert, huh?"

"Yeah… and a gift for you. I told you this was a celebration."

***

The man had serious taste, and his choice of *Eric Roberson in Concert* was right down my alley. When we entered the Music Box, I was almost too nervous to move. It was shaping up to be a really nice night, and I wasn't sure what was coming next. Then *Couldn't Hear Me* started and I broke out of my stupor to dance in the aisle with Jack.

I was pleasantly surprised by him. His moves were fluid and elegant. He was quick and light on his feet. He really knew how to move his hips and reminded me of some of the guys in those South African house music videos that I was hooked on since studying abroad.

His finesse also brought to mind something that I once overheard my grandma Sadie say.

"Don't underestimate them petite men. They don't have a whole lot of extra weight to throw around, and they are efficient with what they got."

By petite she meant any slim man under six feet.

"Honey, 5-foot-anything for a man is petite." she would say.

Basically, Grandma Sadie believed that all petite men were particularly agile in bed. She highly valued precision over power, even though a preference for very tall men ran in the family.

Jack kept his hands in all the appropriate places, and managed to embrace me with a warmth that made him seem safe, unassuming and reassuring. When the concert ended, my defenses were completely dismantled.

***

The redhead was a talented designer who Jack had enlisted to redesign our room for the night, and she was worth every dollar plus tips. She transformed what was already a very nice Water Club suite into a posh, modern, almost ethereal lair.

Soft, ambient music played as we walked in. Two rows of glass vases— which must have been over four feet tall— lined the walls of the entryway. Vibrant, red ginger flowers sloped out of their tops, as if the floral design guru Jeff Leatham himself had bestowed his signature style upon the room. A few strategically placed, large pillar candles glowed against the fog colored walls. There were colorful, abstract paintings and sculptures throughout along with slick modern furniture.

In the main space, a stainless steel bucket on a table by the bed held two bottles of South African champagne next to a covered platter. In the spa bathroom, the heated, marble surround bathtub was full of Jasmine Vanilla bubble bath.

I couldn't resist touching the bed with its tantalizing cotton-cashmere sheets and linen duvet. Then I got lost in those pillows. There was an array of them, in a gradation of shades from gray to white, all neatly stacked one in front of the other. I wondered if Jack's place was anything like this and thought for a split second that I had really been missing out in all my resistance of his advances.

I guess it looked like I had forgotten he was even in the room with me. I got so cozy on the bed that I kicked off my shoes, closed my eyes and started drifting off while he checked his messages.

Feeling a flirtatious pinch on my arm, I awakened again when he said,

"Oh, that's how it is, huh!" he joked. "You ate and had a good time. Now you just gon' go to sleep on a brotha."

"That would be the logical conclusion as far as I'm concerned." I said, knowing full well that I was pretty much okay with whatever he had in mind.

"You know how late it is. Are you suggesting that something is now *owed* to you?"

He smiled and said, "You know I didn't mean it like that."

"What *did* you mean, cuz I doubt you wanna sit up and watch movies."

I shifted my body to face him head on, cuing to him that I was finally willing to hear his answer.

He hesitated then smiled.

"I told you I had a present for you. Why don't you go in the bathroom and see what it is."

"Okay, this must be really good." I thought.

Why else would he risk killing the mood to send me into the bathroom for some surprise that I may or may not like?

Maybe he could sense that I was only beginning to warm up to him and that a little more thawing was needed to get me right where he wanted me. I was intrigued by his patience and the deliberate manner in which he had obviously planned everything. It made me fully aware of the fact that I had his undivided attention, and that I'd probably had it for quite some time.

I went into the bathroom and immediately noticed a black mesh chemise hanging behind the door.

"Uh oh!" cried a voice within me as I processed what was actually about to happen.

Now I could play along, or I could pretend like I wasn't impressed by his quite graceful attempt at romance and single-handedly destroy a great evening. I decided that if my first time wouldn't be perfect with wedding bells, vows pulled from *Song of Solomon,* and God's approval, it could at least be perfectly pleasurable.

I had given in, but I couldn't resist throwing in a joke before changing.

"Hmmm, I'ma need a drink before I put this on for *you!"*

"I got all that covered!" he yelled right back as I rolled my eyes with a smile.

Nerves kicked in again as I looked in the mirror.

"You better hurry up and get outta this bathroom before the super sweat starts and you have to explain why you're standing in a puddle!"

The sweat could be unrelenting if I did not calm down. It was a real weakness. In any situation where my poker face veiled my nervousness, the sweat could give it away if I wasn't careful. It was a challenge that I had already defeated a couple of times that night.

"Good thing you shaved."

That was totally a hygiene move, but it could be a plus in this situation— unless Jack was one of those older guys who was on the bandwagon when hair was in.

"Oh god, you look like a friggin five-year-old!"

I had to get out of that mirror. I didn't know if the surprise was the chemise or the bubble bath or the whole kit and caboodle, but I figured a quick dip would be a good idea. Maybe he'd join me.

"He can't if you don't get up and unlock the door."

"Shoot!"

I got out of the tub, dried off and rushed to get the bobby pins out of my updo.

I had honed the art of erotic suppression long before I met Jack. Every effort he made at getting me to accept him as anything more than a client had failed. My inner receptionist had blocked all his attempts at entry and provided the protection I needed from his magnetism— or so I thought. Despite all my untrustworthy feelings, it had been easy to ignore him until now.

But this was his territory, and he had mastered the art of attracting me.

It was so late, maybe the inner receptionist was sleeping. Some shady chick with questionable boundaries and a thing for cowhide stilettos was filling in for her, and she was instigating this whole thing. Before I knew it, I was emerging from the bathroom with my locs down and the perfectly fitting chemise clinging to my athletic frame.

"He's still dressed?" I asked myself as I walked back toward the bed. *"Great, now I'm REALLY on display!"*

He had turned the music down slightly and was standing in the window observing the ocean view with a glass of champagne in his hand. Before I could reach out my hand to touch his shoulder, he turned around.

"I knew that would look perfect on you."

I modeled a bit, admiring my reflection in the French doors.

"I gotta say you did pick a winner."

"Of course I did." he said smiling back at me. He set his glass down and stepped closer.

"I guess you finally stopped thinking I was a dirty ol' man."

"I never really thought you were one of those guys. I guess I just figured you'd get over it soon enough and move on to something else. There's plenty of fish in the sea, right?"

He leaned back slightly and gave me an inquisitive look. Then he came even closer and gently placed his hands on my waist. The slight chill in the air completely dissipated with his embrace and I calmed down.

"Maybe you think that because you're used to guys coming to you. But I know it's not easy to find somebody real."

I rolled my eyes again, waiting to hear something that didn't sound so generic and rehearsed.

"You're not naïve, I know that. You ain't no chump, but you're still innocent, all heart. You couldn't live any other way."

He lifted my chin slightly, looked into my reticent eyes with that dark, smoldering stare, and continued.

"Whatever you've seen hasn't made you tough. You might be having a rough time right now, but you're durable. You're timeless— like me. You *are* me. That's why you can't resist being mine."

He rose from leaning on the door then started to walk toward the bedroom. When he realized that I was still stunned by his assessment of me, he turned back and slowly took my hand.

***

My type had always been tall (the taller the better) and beefy— like at least 6′-3″, 200+ pounds kind of beefy.

I liked the strong, silent-but-smart types who could stand next to me in a pair of shades, not say a word, and make me feel like I was being lead around by the Secret Service. At least that was how I imagined it.

Jack had surprised me the moment I met him, because, though he lacked that towering physicality, his presence was no less commanding. He oozed deep strength and quiet confidence and seemed to immediately know anything, everything, especially about me. Then he opened his mouth to speak and showed that he was a really dynamic guy with brains, a sense of humor, and serious charisma. He was friendly, familiar, funny, and fine.

I was shocked by how strong he felt in my arms. For a guy who looked so trim in his crisp, tailored clothing, he was very defined underneath. The size and roughness of his hands, his fingers when compared to mine showed his superior strength and proportions. There was a solid quality to his shoulders, arms and chest which almost felt like extreme tension, but which must have instead been a manifestation of his steely nature. He was way too calm and self-assured to be tense.

At first his heart beat slowly on my cheek. The touch of his hand against my inner thigh was barely a touch at all. It was just enough to rouse my senses and leave them plenty of time to reach back.

When he could see that my senses were fully engaged, his touch progressed from light and deliberate to firm and grounding— a tracing of my waist with his fingers before his hand rested on the small of my back, an unyielding grip on the back of my thigh as he lifted my leg slightly.

Thankfully, it was nothing like all that frantic squeezing and squirming I'd seen in all those love scenes where people seemed to move just for the sake of doing something.

Jack revealed that he was not afraid of time. We both used it as an opportunity to tune in more deeply, to become instant experts on one another.

***

I stared out the window in serene silence as flurries began falling onto the beach. For some reason, I didn't want to talk immediately. I wanted to simply process what had just happened. And I was still in such a good mood that I thought talking would ruin it. But Jack seemed a little unnerved by my brief silence.

"You mighty quiet."

"I'm just…takin' in the scenery." I said with a sigh. "It's the first time I've had a chance to notice anything else all night."

"Oh, I thought you were gradin' me."

"Grading you?"

"Comparing me to all the other guys you've been with and deciding my grade."

I burst out laughing.

"Are you serious?"

"I know y'all women do that stuff."

"That was not even where my head was… but I guess you still wanna know your *grade*, huh?"

He was clearly expecting an assessment.

"Well..." I said, "you tell me my grade. I'm the one who's the student."

Jack look perplexed, shook his head like he didn't understand, then said, "Yeeeah right!"

"What?" I asked, indignantly

"You ain't gotta front with me. I'm not judgmental. But I know you not tryin' to tell me that was your f— "

He instantly changed his tone from playful to a little more compassionate when he saw no joke on my face.

I rolled my eyes and looked back out the window.

"So?" He asked, nuzzling up next to me. Whether or not his assumption was correct, he still wanted to know how he did.

I hadn't expected my first time to be even slightly good. I thought it would be more like a trial run with plenty of fumbling and mutual embarrassment.

That was one thing that helped me to resist the temptation for so long. I figured most of the guys I came into contact with probably got all their sexual pointers from porn and friends who were just as clueless as them. They may have gotten around, but I assumed they weren't any more adept in the art of sensuality than the average virgin. I figured I wasn't missing much.

The High Art of Sensuality was what my good friend, Devi, liked to call it. It was that connection with one's own sexuality, that patience and cultivated understanding of timing, conscious, nuanced touch, and the ability to listen to another person's body which made one adept.

I could see exactly what she meant that night. There was, however, one thing that she and many of my other well-meaning elders said in an effort to spoil the prospect of premature sex which turned out to be a brazen lie.

It was the notion that sex could only be good with someone you love. Actually, as I learned that night, sex could be quite enjoyable with somebody you barely knew. It was a force far beyond anybody's ability to control or define. And according to other conversations that I had no business hearing as a child, it could be spectacular with someone you didn't even like and completely boring and played out with the love of your life. Go figure.

***

The next morning, I awakened to the scent of Jack's cologne still lingering on the sheets. I glanced at the clock and saw that it was already nearing noon. Sleepy and hypnotized I followed the fragrance, clutching the sheets hand-over-hand until I found jack underneath them on the other side of the bed. He was checking his emails on his phone.

"You know as much as I hate to leave, we should probably head back to Philly soon. I have a few things to do today before I go home for Christmas break."

"I know." he said without looking up.

"You know what?"

"I know you always got *something* to do. How long you gon' be in Virginia?"

"I-I guess probably until…for the whole break, I guess."

I still hadn't made up my mind about that. This little overnight had provided much of the relief I was after when I first planned to set aside a few dollars for an extended getaway. I was never able to save the money, but I still considered asking an old friend near the beach if I could crash on her sofa while she spent the holiday out of town.

"Why, you gonna be lonely while I'm gone?"

He smiled and took one of my hands in his.

"I just might be… you ready for next semester?"

"As ready as can be expected."

Just the thought of school was enough to throw me back into exhaustion.

"Well," Jack said, "your professor said you told him you were thinking about taking the semester off."

"You talked to my professor about *that*?"

"It wasn't like I was all in yo' business, but I saw him in center city one day. He asked how your work for me was going, and we talked a lil' bit."

I closed my eyes and turned away from him.

"What else did he say?"

"Not a whole lot, other than that he didn't really doubt that you'd be okay. He figured if you took a break, you'd be that much better off when you go back."

Jack rubbed my back and tried to help me relax.

"Either way, I asked him to give you a lil' boost."

"What?"

"I asked him to help you out."

"Huh?"

"I gave him a lil' holiday bonus and asked him to turn that hard C you were about to get into a slight A. That'll help your GPA a little, right?"

"He didn't go along with that, did he?"

"Why wouldn't he? He's not even tenure-track, he can use the money. Lemme know when you check your grades."

"Who the heck does this negro think he is?"

One day he's wining and dining me, the next he's bribing my professors? Before I could figure out a way to avoid utter academic ruin in the wake of this stunt, he revealed another one while slowly pulling me in closer and kissing the palm of my hand.

"And I made a deposit in your account this morning. I know you would rather not be working those other two jobs. You might as well just quit and free up some study time. If you take the semester off, maybe you can take the time you woulda been working and get in some more CAD practice, go over some of the other stuff you don't have a lot of time to study, at your own pace. If you change your mind about working for me, the offer's still on the table."

I was in shock. I couldn't do anything but sit there with my mouth hanging open and wonder what was happening.

"How did you get access to my bank account?" I asked, yanking my hand away from his mouth.

"Calm down, girl! Your checkbook is in your purse. I got it while you were sleepin'."

"You went in my purse?"

"After last night you got a problem with me bein' in your *purse*?"

For the first time, I was speechless. There was something very wrong with this situation. In fact, it was all wrong. We weren't even, technically, in a relationship yet and he had assumed a permanent position in my life as academic mediator and benefactor.

"What is it?" he asked.

I didn't answer and turned to get out of the bed.

He grabbed my arm.

"I know what's bothering you. You think you cheated. You think you cheated, and it's not right, and somebody's gonna find out, and it's gonna ruin everything. Just act like you didn't know— it's not like *you* asked him to change the grade."

I stayed quiet.

"Jane, you need to understand that those kids you're competing with, those trust fund babies who've been working in their uncle's firms since they were fourteen—even they cheat. So you don't stand a chance if you keep takin' the long, hard, moral road."

He brushed aside my hair and gently placed his chin on my shoulder.

"I'm giving you an advantage. You deserve it. Take it."

I hoped to God that my professor knew Jack and I well enough to understand that the bribe was all Jack's idea.

***

We sat in front of my building for a minute, and I tried to make goodbye quick but sweet. The rest of the afternoon would be a blur until dinner at Jessica's. It was already 3:15 and I had to make the spice mix for the roast which I had not marinated, cook everything, and transport the food to Jessica's apartment.

This was all the more reason for me to avoid letting Jack come up to my apartment to finish our goodbye kiss. Plus I still hadn't invited him to dinner and wasn't planning to. After everything that just happened I needed a breather from him, and I definitely didn't want to have to introduce him to all my friends that day.

He could hardly care less that I was stressing.

"You're gonna be gone in a few days. This could be the last time we see each other for weeks."

"I know, Jack, but I really have to get some things in order before I go. Then I wanna just get some down time before the drive."

I avoided making eye contact with him, knowing that I would miss him now more than I ever had. Confusion was something I rarely felt, but the conflict between my feelings for him and my suspicion of him was intensifying.

I knew that my mom would notice if I went home with this much on my mind. If my poker face failed or my inability to lie remained consistent, she would quickly sniff out the figurative scent of a man and call for a cleansing prayer. This could even prompt another suggestion that I leave school for the wrong reasons. The idea of another hiatus, one in pure solitude, was becoming more attractive by the minute.

He relieved the tension in my neck by rubbing his thumb in an upward motion toward my ear and didn't say a word. Despite our overt attraction, he still leaned toward subtlety when he was actually asking me to have sex with him. He wasn't demanding— he knew that ultimately, he didn't have to be.

Something in me said," *How long is it really gonna take to stick a roast in the oven. You're mostly gonna be sitting around waiting for it to cook... Of course, then he'll ask why you're cooking and he'll want to stay for dinner and—"*

Just then, I could see Irving in the distance carrying two handfuls of groceries down Greene Street. I was not about to explain to Jack why some guy was dropping groceries off at my place or why he was coming up to my apartment and would be staying until I gave him a ride back to campus for the dinner. It would probably not be a good scene.

So I stiffened up and gave Jack one last kiss, then looked into his eyes to reassure him,

"I'll call you tonight."

"Okay." he said without any push back. With a secure and peaceful grin on his face, he got out and opened my door.

7

"Guess who brought grilled fish and attieke?!"

Giselle pushed the door open with her back then swung around with a broad smile and that characteristic high look in her eyes. I leaned against the wall and swooned at the thought of adding a scoop of the shredded cassava dish to my plate.

"Where did you get it?" Jessica demanded. "Cuz you didn't cook it and you didn't buy it!"

"Jesus, Jess!" Giselle shot back while standing frozen with the heavy food still in her hands.

"So what if I didn't cook it? You asked us to bring something."

"Is that man buying you stuff again? You better be careful with him."

"For your information, I made the fish and Anodiwa made the attieke."

"You got it at Le Mandique, didn't you?" Jessica asked, completely ignoring what Giselle said. "There's no need for lying!"

I raised my eyebrows at the mention of Giselle's on again off again, quasi-married boyfriend buying her stuff. I quickly poured a glass of Moscato and skulked off to the living room.

Anodiwa shuffled past me and into the kitchen in order to second Giselle's claim. Her slow, easy movement, the sentimental tilt of her head, and the comforting loose layers which she preferred not to pull off all showed her typical melancholy.

"We actually did cook the food, Jessica."

"Oh my god!" Jessica said rounding them up for a hug. "You young ladies are growing up. I'm so proud of you. Did you taste test it?"

The noise from the kitchen faded as I tuned in to my phone to check my messages. After I took the phone away from my ear Irving leaned in to tell me something in a hush.

"While Jessica's makin' her rounds, I thought I'd warn you. I know you probably showered… but you still smell like him."

I looked at him in shock then peeked around him to make sure nobody was eavesdropping.

Shaking his head slightly, he went on,

"No no no. It's cologne. I can tell it's nice cologne, but it's *cologne*. It's in your hair."

"Why didn't you tell me that before you fell asleep on my couch for two hours?!"

"I thought maybe he visited your apartment. I didn't know the scent was coming from *you*."

As the kitchen conversation shifted from Anodiwa's refusal to remove her favorite hat to the question of whether Giselle was still on the pill, I tried to calm down.

"So what? I hugged him. I hug plenty of people and walk away smelling like their perfume."

"Yeah. That must have been… a long hug."

I immediately got up, hustled to the bathroom and started looking for something to help mask the smell. I figured I would just dampen my hair lightly and mist on a little of Jessica's body spray before drying it. It hardly mattered, though, because I knew Jessica had already caught a good whiff of it when we greeted at the door. She was probably just saving the best for last.

"Where is this child's blow dryer?"

It was nowhere to be found— not on the counter, in the cubby above the toilet, the linen closet, or under the sink. When I realized that I was losing way too much of my cool, I stepped back and looked in the mirror.

"What are you doing? You were gonna tell your girls anyway, so chill out."

"Yeah, but I was hoping to tell them on my own terms." I said under my breath as I gave up and walked back toward the living room.

As I started down the hall, Giselle came bursting out of the kitchen with her hands in the air and mouthing, "What the heck" at Ryan and Irving.

Jessica followed right behind her and shouted, "CONDOMS!" loud enough for everybody in her place and a few people outside to hear.

I backpedaled and walked into a bedroom instead.

The doorbell rang and everything went quiet for a minute. I figured it was Rashida and tried to cheer myself up with the thought of adding her cornbread to my plate.

Then Celine came rushing into the bedroom, removing her shirt as she talked.

"It is too hot! I dunno why I decided to wear three shirts. It's colder than a witch's tit outside and a sauna in here."

"What's going on out there?" I asked. "Has the inquisition cooled off yet?"

"Nope. That's still hot too, my dear. Jessica was out there lecturing everybody bout condoms, Shawn keeps eyeballing Rashida, and your man just walked through the door with two more bottles of Merlot."

"WHAT?!"

"He's out there."

She said that so nonchalantly that I had to remind her that Jack's presence could not be possible.

"I did not invite him."

"He invited himself. Merry Christmas."

"How did he find Jessica's place?"

Giselle stood in the doorway with the first plate to be made that evening.

"Is she serious?!" Giselle complained about Jessica's interrogation. "I mean, I know what I'm doing. I understand her concern, but here? Now?! I'd like to find the skeletons in *her* closet, you know? Geez."

Celine and I looked at each other. Sensing a minor alert, Celine looked back at Giselle and said,

"You know how Jessica is. You betta get that food out of this bedroom."

Giselle wasn't fooled by our attempt to cut her out of the secret.

"What's wrong?"

"I'm not sure yet." I said as I brushed past her and walked out of the bedroom.

"There she *i-is*." Jessica sang as I emerged from the hallway and approached the couch. Jack was seated in between Ryan and Irving, apparently having a very engaging conversation.

I smiled and politely reached for his arm. He stood up and followed me into the kitchen.

"What is this?" I asked.

"What *is* it? Look like y'all gettin' ready to eat to me. That's some really good wine I picked up, by the way. I think you'll like it."

He was absolutely shameless, and I had no idea what to do with him. I started piling food on his plate and he said,

"You know I was feeling some kinda way when I saw Irving go into your apartment with you… but now I get it. I just don't understand why you couldn't invite me."

"Because I wasn't ready for you to be here, Jack!" I blurted out. "What am I supposed to call you?"

"Yeah, what are you supposed to call me?"

I banged the serving spoon on the plate a couple of times to remove a stubborn bit of bread pudding. Jack reached for the spoon.

I said in resistance, "I can put the food on the plate."

He insisted, "I'm just saying, I can make my own plate."

I rebutted, "Well, I already started *making* the plate, Jack!"

He looked at me as if he was both surprised and amused by my anger.

"Alright, young buck. You know, I don't eat much red meat, but since you made it I gotta try it."

I slapped a piece of roast beef onto the plate, shoved it into his chest and turned him toward the living room.

I sat there for two and a half hours and endured watching him pry into the good graces of every single person in the room. He complimented the ladies on the cooking and shared ingredients from his own late mother's recipes. He asked Jessica for a recommendation on a good chiropractor for his foot. He cracked jokes with the guys. At one point, they even went running outside so Irving could take a go behind the wheel of Jack's Jaguar XKR.

"I don't drink," Irving panted, "so I haven't had anything but soda tonight. I *promise* I won't crash your car, man!"

After they got back and we all settled into our seats with dessert, a news flash about a murder in North Philly came on TV.

"Authorities say the body of a man who was shot late Friday night has been found in the Nicetown section of North Philadelphia… The victim has been identified as twenty-three-year-old Seymour Clancy."

The man's name didn't register for me until the camera panned to one of Seymour's neighbors who seemed nonchalant about the news.

"I mean, he did his own thing, you know. He ain't bother nobody. He did odd jobs and stuff. I used to pay him to cut my grass. He cut grass up the street, too. And I heard he did some work for this cat that's into real estate. You know, he did have a

lil' drug problem, so... that coulda had somethin' to do with it. Maybe he owed somebody."

"Lurch!" I said under my breath when they showed a recent photo of him.

I elbowed Jack and asked him if he had heard anything about this before seeing the report.

"Nah, that's news to me. But I ain't surprised."

He threw another piece of cake in his mouth.

"Told you that boy had a problem. Ain't a problem for me no more, though."

***

When it was time for everyone to go home, I played it cool and helped Jessica clean up. While she raved about what a good guest Jack had been and what an interesting guy he must be I kept cutting my eyes at him.

He was absolutely unruffled by the news of Seymour's death. He had also been equally undaunted by the fact that I was uncomfortable with the way he had barged into my life over the last couple of days. I had made the mistake of letting him in and he wasn't going to go away easily or voluntarily.

"I think he killed somebody."

"What?" Jessica put down a soapy glass and turned off the water.

"Turn it back on! Somebody might hear." I stood close to Jessica and lowered my voice.

"Well, maybe he didn't kill him, but I think he might have had something to do with someone's death."

"Jane, why would you think something like that?"

"That boy, that boy that was just on the news, he used to work for Jack."

"Oh my god, that's terrible. But what reason would he have for—"

"He told me that the boy tried to steal from him before."

"And Jack is a cold-blooded, gangster real estate investor who would go after somebody like that and have him killed? Come on, Jane. The boy was a drug addict."

She pointed at me with suds dripping from her index finger.

"You are scared because you don't want to believe that Jack's really in love with you. You don't want to believe it's possible. And I know he may be coming on a little strong now, but that may be what it takes to get your attention."

She stopped washing dishes again and looked at my confused face.

"I know what probably happened between you and him this weekend, Jane. But he seems like a really great guy who's got a lot going for him and he wants to include you. You shouldn't let your fears spoil that. If you're really happy when you're with him, why try and run now?"

There was, undoubtedly, a part of me that wanted to relax and just enjoy Jack. He clearly had a way of making me forget all my life's drama. And the assumption of murder was a bit of a stretch.

Even though I was fifteen years his junior, I got the sense that I was still a challenge for him and that he liked that. A lot of guys say they love a smart woman until they actually have to talk to one, but Jack wasn't turned off by intellect. He saw it as one of my greatest assets.

In him I had the best of two worlds: the energy, zest for life and raw ambition of someone my age and the patience and maturity of someone older and more experienced.

As he stood next to his car searching for his car keys, I told him, "You absolutely cannot do anything like this again."

"Okay, I know— even though I've done everything possible to let you know I'm in your corner, and even though you clearly don't mind me crossing the line sometimes. I won't just be all up in your business like that. You got a right to your business."

"Are you sure, Jack? This has to slow down. I'm not saying I don't want to be with you… but the freight train has got to slow down. I want you to talk to my professor tomorrow morning and *take back* that request you made."

He lifted his hands in surrender.

"You betta not let that man drive!" Jessica yelled from her window.

If it had not been for her, I might have considered taking that chance. I couldn't be alone in a car with him after softening on him again. I hoped the little alcohol he drank had relaxed his brain enough to make him a little less cunning.

"Why don't we just go to your place?" he said as I started the car.

So much for my hopes.

"Too late for you to be driving around. I know you had a glass."

"One glass. I'm hardly inebriated." I said.

"Jane, it's late and you have to travel soon. I don't thinks it's a good idea for you to drive me all the way to Bucks County right now and then drive all the way back here. I'm keeping my promise, alright?"

***

Jack went to sleep shortly after we got to my place, and I stayed up to get my keys when Irving dropped off my car.

When Irving came to the door, he butted his head into my entryway and looked toward the couch. Then he looked back at me.

"Here are your keys, Ms. Jane. My roommate's waiting for me downstairs."

"Okay." I said wondering why he wasn't hurrying back down to meet him. He must have known Jack was in my bedroom.

"I can see that… Jack's beautiful car is parked on the side street just outside your building."

"Okay." I said.

He put his hands in his pockets and nodded.

"Well… you seem unbothered so I… hope you have a good night and a safe trip home."

"Yeah, you too, Irving. I hope you enjoy your holiday. Thanks a lot for dropping off my car."

"*No* problem, Jane. God bless."

He started to walk away and stopped to say one more thing.

"You missed church today, Jane." He raised his finger and repeated himself, "You missed *church* today."

"Seriously?" I thought. *"Get the hell out of here!"*

Shady Chick must have still been on duty. I nodded graciously then rolled my eyes as I slammed and locked the door.

Then I slid into bed behind Jack and hesitantly cozied up next to him. I really wanted to snuggle up in front of him in perfect spoonion, but decided not to for obvious reasons.

Didn't matter though. The moment I wrapped my arm around his waist he woke up and turned over to face me.

"Ay." he whispered.

"Hey back."

"You can come closer."

"You sure?"

"I'm keeping my promise."

I smiled and settled with Jack into an embrace that left no empty space between our bodies or our hearts.

8

At 3am I woke up to the sound of my phone vibrating on the small table next to my bed. It was my counselor-friend, Devi.

What was she doing calling this late, or this early? She lived in Arizona, which meant that she was two hours behind my time. She was also known for being a night owl, but this was just bizarre.

I decided to pick up, because I knew she wouldn't call me at such an odd hour for anything frivolous. Deep down I also knew that I was in need of the wisdom of this woman who was more than twice my age.

I leaned into the living room closet and answered the phone.

"Who is this man chasing you?"

"Huh? Devi, did you have another dream? You sound groggy?"

"I wanted to check on you. You haven't called me in a while."

"I know."

I felt guilty for letting so much time go between our calls, but I didn't feel right taking up so much of her time when I didn't always have the means to pay her. In my mind, she was my counselor when I was able to pay her and my friend when I wasn't. I didn't want to take advantage of a friend.

"I was going to give you a call right after I got home for break. How have you been?"

She took a deep breath and shifted from slightly disoriented to the serene tone of a seasoned Life Coach.

"I've been well. How have *you* been?" she asked.

"Well, I'm ready for a much-needed break. It'll be good to see family and my friends back home. I need the change of scenery to blow some fresh air into my routine and help me recharge."

"Yeah." she continued slowly. She sounded like she was searching my tone in order to hear what I was not yet telling her. Or maybe I was just paranoid.

"I think time off is best for you. And you should have some fun, you know? Go out with your girlfriends, spend some time at the beach you love so much, take in the scenery and the beautiful ocean. You're young, you shouldn't be so serious all the time. People think I'm old and I still know that I should be having fun!"

I laughed with her but was careful to keep my voice low.

"And you might want to take it easy with the men for a while. Don't do anything you're not ready to do. No pressure. The last thing you need right now is pressure."

Now her intuition was kicking in, and I could feel something coming on that was less lecture, more premonition. I couldn't ignore it.

"Your father..."

"Oh! Thank goodness." I thought. *"On to another topic."*

"Has he been acting out lately?"

"Yeah, he got into a big fight with my brother not too long ago. It was pretty nasty. They got into a screaming match outside my grandma's house and somebody almost called the cops. It went to blows but my dad was so drunk, Terrence ended it pretty quick."

"Mmm... that must be why he keeps coming up for me. What about your mom?"

"She married that guy."

"...Oh my... Well, I called you because I want you to be extra mindful while you're away. There will be plenty of time for you to hear yourself think, and I think it will be a real opportunity to make progress in some of the areas we talked about, if you pay attention."

"Devi, what did you see?"

I just knew that she had another one of her dreams and, considering the circumstances, I was getting nervous.

"What are you worried about?" she said in that playful and reassuring tone she always used when I was crying, snotting and at the edge of my wits, all while she was having a glass of wine with her feet up on the other end.

"Don't you think I'm telling you everything you need to know? There's no use for fear anyway. You know, what you fear will come upon you."

Fear was something we had really been working on. In all the journaling that I did over the years, I discovered

that there was this undercurre
underneath most of my decisions—
rejection, fear of being alone, f
parents' shortcomings, fear of pis
worst possible outcome in whatev

I had enlisted Devi to help me unpack the su
roots of those fears and reprogram my mind toward a more positive disposition.

She went on, "Sometimes these things are figurative. I could simply be tuning in to your mood, picking up on your emotions. We've made such a connection, Jane. You're so much like me when I was younger. But you're a seeker. You'll find your way, and I'll help you."

We continued our talk for almost an hour. I told her about how, at one point, I went to the free on campus counselor to see if she had any insight to offer as I juggled school, work, and life.

"I don't know what it was, but she seemed clueless, Devi. I told her about some of the things that were bothering me and about how my grades were slipping, how my head was a sleepy jumble. She just looked at me. She stuttered and stammered and just looked at me like I was from *Mars*. She didn't seem at all interested in getting to know me, trying to understand me. It was like talking to a wall. She didn't offer any coping strategies or suggestions. I felt completely uncomfortable, so I just thanked her and left after a few minutes. I got this pamphlet for adult ADHD on the way out. For a few days, I thought I had it!"

"Jane," Devi said with a chuckle, "girl, you do not have ADHD. Sounds like that woman was probably ill-equipped to be in a counseling position. Who knows where they got her from. And the schools can't stop at

.g y'all blood and sweat for tuition, food, and s? They wanna let in the pharmaceutical companies they can pump a bunch of college students full of ADHD meds, too?"

"Well, she looked like some clueless library mouse—they must have picked her out of a Lancaster farmhouse somewhere. She probably never even heard of crack cocaine or the projects."

"Okay, Jane."

"Shoulda never told her my business! Probably didn't know what to do with a po' black girl in her office. Looked at me like I was from Mars!"

"Alright, Jane."

"Woman looked like Olive Oyl from the *Popeye* cartoons."

"Olive Oyl? Really, Jane? Let's get back on track. There's no need to insult the woman. And why are you talking so low?"

"Hmm?"

"You are almost whispering. Your crazy neighbor been complaining about noise from your place again?"

"Uh, no, not lately."

"Then why don't you speak up, girl?" Devi was never one to behave impatiently, but she had had enough.

"Um… I have company."

"…Oh, you tryin' to keep from waking *him* up, huh?"

She laughed out loud, almost as if teasing me because I couldn't.

"That's why you haven't called me lately, cuz you been runnin' around with this slick new man."

"What makes you think he's slick?"

"He's sleeping in your bed, isn't he? He *got* to be made of coconut oil!"

After thoroughly enjoying a few more laughs, Devi let out one big sigh and said,

"Don't let him own you. You know that's what he wants. Security is fine. Sovereignty is better."

I was a little embarrassed to know that Devi's premonition may have revealed even more about me and Jack than she was telling. Even still, I fully accepted her advice.

"Okay, so lemme ask you something." I said quickly.

I didn't want to stall and allow my shyness to keep me from asking a burning question.

"When we were... together... for the first time— you know it was my first time— something happened that I've never really heard of before."

"Um hmm." Devi said.

"Ya know, everybody's always talking about this big... main event that's supposedly the be-all and end-all of the sexual experience."

The receptionist was beginning to resurface as I coded my language in an attempt to avoid disrespecting an elder.

"That didn't happen. Not in the way everybody says. Well, it wasn't an explicit... localized... sensation. It was really strange, like it was all over, and it didn't really intensify until afterwards when we were just lying there."

"Um hmm." Devi said.

"Is that afterglow, because it's still happening!"

"Well, if you would give me a few more details, I could help you figure that out."

She seemed annoyed. Her sensibilities were probably not as fragile as I had assumed.

"Okay." I said. "This must be what it feels like to be high. It's like a completely physical yet nonphysical sensation. I've never done drugs, so I don't know, but that's the only way I can describe it. It's like all my cells are vibrating. If I stop for a second and just get quiet, I can feel this pulsating energy all over my body. It's like extreme relaxation but more than that. It's like my hands and feet are coming alive. My eyes and ears feel like they're being massaged from the inside out. There's this warm feeling in the center of my core that just keeps growing. At first this surge of… something just shot up to my head like buzzing electricity. Now my head feels light, and alive, like it's expanding. I feel really clear and energized. Not spacy at all— totally clear and calm and happy. It first started after we kissed the first time. I expected it to knock the wind right out of me, but instead it seemed to fill me with energy. It was like a subtle charge infusing me with vitality!"

I lifted my head and closed my eyes to take in the sensations then snapped back to reality when she spoke.

"That's a full body orgasm."

"What? Full body?"

"Um hmm."

She knew more— a lot more. I suspected she was holding back to avoid indulging my curiosity, but the cat was already out of the bag.

"It's called a full body orgasm. Those can last for hours… Get rid of him."

"I knew that man had mojo!" I whisper-shouted.

"Something about the experience made you open to it. Under the right circumstances that can happen without any physical contact or proximity. It's not him. It's you, Jane. *He's* got to go!"

I smiled and stared at my hands as if I was becoming aware of some latent superpower.

"You hear me, Jane? When he wakes up, get him outta there."

She issued my next assignment in the sweetest and most motherly of tones.

"Send that man home first thing in the morning, and focus on making the most of your trip. Stay safe and take your time. I want you to really think about the sequence of events that led to this predicament you're in and ask yourself if any of it looks familiar."

"Predicament? This doesn't feel like a predicament."

She continued, "Don't let yourself get distracted. Sometimes a change of scenery can give you great perspective."

I could hear her scratching down notes in the background.

"I want you to keep a journal on your trip. However long you may be away, use that time to think about what's happening and the patterns of thinking that led you here. You also should think about the men you've spent time with over the last few years and what motivated you to become involved. And when you take an honest look at the outcome of the choices you've made, I think you'll be well equipped to move forward in a better way. I could tell you all the answers, but sometimes experience is the best teacher. Be safe, and take care. I love you."

"Thank you. I love you, too, Devi. Good morning!"

***

Just after sunrise, I went downstairs to the laundry room to wash some clothes. When I got back to my apartment and approached the bedroom, Jack was there talking on his cell phone and putting a handgun in his pants with his back to the doorway. Just before he pulled his shirt down over it I saw what looked like a bunch of messy lines scratched into the metal, where, I assumed, the serial number should be.

"I'on know what you tellin' me for, Man. The boy been dead since Friday. I ain't been up that way for over a week … That ain't my problem. *You* 'sposed to fix that shit. Call me when you fix it."

When he hung up I quickly turned around and shoved my towels into the linen closest just outside the bedroom.

"Hey, girl! I didn't even know you were in here. Why you runnin' around this early in the morning?"

I acted like I hadn't seen or heard a thing.

"I told you, I want to get all these errands out of the way so I can leave soon. I wanna avoid night driving, with the ice and all."

"You know what I should do?"

He hugged my waist and kissed me on the forehead.

"I should just buy you a plane ticket to Norfolk. You won't have to waste time doing all that driving."

"Really, it's fine, Jack. I love taking the drive, it's relaxing. And I'll need my car while I'm there."

"I could get you a rental."

"What about your promise?"

"Okay, whatever. Well you'll be happy to know I sent your professor an email a while ago. He said that after the exam, you pretty much got an A anyway."

That would have been really good news if I could be confident that it was actually true. For all I knew, Jack could have been in the middle of cleaning up after one murder and planning to commit another one if my professor didn't bend to his will. I just wanted him out of my place so I could leave town.

"I guess this is goodbye for now." he said.

He stood with his back to the front door and held out his arms for a hug. I stepped toward him slowly and locked my fingers behind his back in a sincere embrace. It wasn't long before my head began to drop under the weight of another orgasmic surge. Fortunately, he broke the silence with a goodbye kiss and left, in keeping with his promise.

***

Before filling up my gas tank and hitting the road, I needed to stop at the ATM down the street. I would really miss this place, even if I would only be gone for a short while.

The October Gallery was moving into to a house across the street. I'd once had my body painted by a talented artist, Deborah Shedrick, at the gallery's annual Philadelphia Art Expo and been a follower ever since.

The tiny A & N House of Produce further down Greene Street, where I got all my fruits and veggies for dirt cheap, allowed me to get by on a college student's budget without destroying my health on that infamous Ramen Noodle diet. (Ending up in the emergency room after another hypoglycemic episode brought on by poor diet was not an option.)

The Ebenezer Maxwell Mansion, three blocks from my building was the spooky and beautiful Victorian house museum where I worked part-time. I spent many Tuesday and Thursday evenings alone in that place, organizing files in the attic, polishing the silver in the dining room, and shining the wood furniture. I helped the wealthy Victorians keep up appearances long after their passing.

The convenience store across from Vernon park where I always stopped for icies in the summer, the Free Library across Chelten Avenue, and Yadain, the Islamic themed cosmetics store where I got all my incense— these were all a part of the cozy, exotic little world I had created for myself. Though school often felt like a cold and foreign place, this, my home was familiar and full of the things that interested me.

I parked on the street and got out to use the ATM. This was always a sort of nerve-wracking experience. God only knew what I was ever likely to find in my account, despite my attempts at fiscal responsibility. How does one maintain a budget when prayer, working for peanuts, and robbing Peter to pay Paul are the underpinnings of their financial strategy?

I had to believe that there was enough in there to get me to Virginia where some generous familial soul would bestow a few more dollars upon me, even though I never felt right asking for it.

"Are those four zeros?"

"Ten thousand dollars?!"

The gentleman behind me gave a look warning me to keep the financial blessing to myself. I looked back at the screen.

"Oh my god! Jack."

In the midst of everything else, I had totally forgotten about the money he said he put in my account! I had assumed it was only a few hundred, not more than a thousand.

I looked around to see if I could spot his car. The situation felt realer than it ever had. I now suspected that Jack had been watching me regularly, I knew that he went around with a gun, that he was trying to get somebody to "fix" something possibly related to a guy's death, and that this money was the most potent tool of all in his scheme to secure my devotion.

Where was he now? If my goodbye kiss had done the trick, he would be somewhere else secure in the understanding that I was completely his… at least until I could figure out my next move.

Part 2

Love is available to all

and beholden to none.

9

I could faintly hear the man's voice nearby.

"Woman, are you crazy?!"

It was barely loud enough to be heard over the waves so I ignored it and continued to bask in the long overdue pleasure of freedom, femininity, and wonder. Though the night air was cool, I was warm beneath the knit throw that I'd grabbed from the ottoman in my bungalow.

It was so nice to feel like a real woman again and to enjoy it without the fog of Jack being attached to it. I sat there with my shoulder-length locs down, wearing a long, white, fitted, scoop neck dress, which had dragged along the sand. I imagined that I looked like a mirage in the night. My bare feet were still covered in sand that I hadn't bothered to wipe off. My only other adornment was a heavy white necklace I had made out of freshwater pearls, wood, and shell beads.

Relaxing at the threshold between sand and bay, I continued to stare into the water. With the full moon lighting the way for me, I settled onto my stomach with a thick yoga mat shielding me from the rough limestone rock beneath it. I nestled my head into my palms, and, staring straight down, waited for answers to roll in on the waves.

"What the hell is wrong with this chick?" I heard him say, as if to himself.

"Oh, Lord." I grumbled under my breath. "Leave it to the ignoramuses to spoil heaven on earth!"

If someone was about to air their stupid lover's quarrel for everyone, I wanted them to know that I was not at all entertained.

"Just put it on YouTube!" I yelled over my shoulder.

"What? Hey… did you hear me calling you? I've been trying to get your attention from the sand down there… The guests called me about you. I'm Officer Stevens with security."

I could hear his pants rubbing together as he rushed up the steps which were roughly cut into the thirty-foot, limestone rock formation that I was lounging on.

He caught his breath then mumbled, "If *this* ain't the dumbest, craziest..."

"Oh… okay." I said to myself as I slowly rose up to brush myself off. Then, while still not looking at him, I quickly mustered up a tight string of backtalk to let the puny rent-a-cop know I didn't need his help.

"Well, I'm sorry people find me so intriguing that they couldn't take their eyes off me from their windows! Heaven forbid you should interrupt snooze time to come over here and do your job!"

"Ain't dis some bull!" he ranted. "You're sitting at the edge of a cliff at night with no one else around. I climb up this damn rock to make sure you're okay, and all I get is insults?"

I said, "You climbed stairs, honey. It was hardly an Olympic challenge. And is it also your job to verbally abuse the people you're *supposed* to protect— because as I recall, you insulted me first!"

I shifted my weight slightly to the left and peered over my right shoulder to give him one good, side-eyed mean mug. What caught me completely off guard was one of the most gorgeous men that I had ever seen in my life.

The man looked almost unreal; so much so that I shook my head and wondered if the moonlight was playing tricks on me, or if my *mind* was.

For two days I had been fasting to achieve inner silence, drinking only fresh fruit juices and avoiding the noise of TV, social media and the constant ringing of my phone. I had spent the last two evenings at the edge of the water, washing away layers of angst. By the looks of that man, I thought maybe I'd broken through the veil and achieved an answer from God. Was this a spirit messenger?

Hoping for some clue that would reveal the nature of his being, I looked at a small puddle of water close to where I sat. There was his reflection on the surface! Still I needed more proof.

I clamored quickly back toward him and grabbed the first thing within my reach— his ankle— which led me up a thick, oak-strong thigh, wrapped in a delicious layer of coal black skin. The shirt and slacks that he wore to shield him from the night air did nothing to hide the powerful, athletic frame beneath. He hesitated then kicked his foot downward just as my hand neared his most treasured area.

His face, precise and intent in expression, glistening in the night, looked as if it had been sculpted in bronze. He had full lips, a sharp nose, high cheekbones, and piercing, almost narrow eyes that seemed buried below thin, naturally contoured brows. His build was lean and ferociously strong. His presence was subtle and mysterious, yet reassuring. I came to my senses just enough to flop back down in total exhausted amazement and ask,

"Where the hell did you come from?"

I slipped out of this trance and realized that I might be the subject of a citizen's arrest.

"Do they do that kind of thing in Bermuda?"

The last thing I wanted was to be forwarded to the local hospital for a psychiatric evaluation.

Then again, he probably thought I was trying to seduce him to get out of trouble for getting smart with him. I released his left bicep in time to make him change his mind about calling the real cops on me.

After settling back down onto my yoga mat, I saw that he was returning a walkie-talkie to his back pocket. Then, after getting another look at his face, I was able to see that he was probably younger than I'd initially assumed. He had the fresh, taut look of a very health- and image-conscious man in his mid-twenties.

He squinted his eyes at me for a few seconds while I adjusted on the mat. Hypoglycemia was kicking in and I felt a slight wave of faintness pass over me as I settled back down. Enough fasting. I needed to go back inside and eat something.

He straightened his back and loosened his shoulders then said in a lowered voice, "Listen, Miss, why don't you let me help you back down? Go ahead back to your bungalow, and stop lying around out here like some drunk. You're lucky I didn't see whatever bottle you've been sippin' from. I was *this* close to calling the cops on you. But I am gonna have to write up a report to security so they can keep an eye on you."

As I chuckled, he gathered what little authority he was able to salvage and started taking notes.

"Hey, you don't have an accent. You're from the states? Can you even see what you're writing?" I asked, peeking onto his paper. He ignored me and quietly led the way back down the steps.

Once back on the sand I asked, "What do I get for feeling you up?"

"You want a trip to the police station!" He snapped.

I smirked, gave him one last look from head to toe and rolled my eyes. "I guess that means you're the boss."

I sashayed off toward my bungalow looking one last time over my shoulder to sing a coy "Good night officer!"

***

As I made my way back to my room, the cadence of the dancing waves as my background music, I thought about Devi's assignment. On the plane, I penciled it in my itinerary. Monday night, along with "Begin reading *The Iliad*" and "try the barracuda at that local Australian restaurant" was "Jane: 2006, A Love Analysis." But I'd been procrastinating on it since I arrived.

Technically, I could say the journal was halfway done. My collection of diary entries, love letters, late night rants, scriptures, travel logs, and inspiring quotes were like a record of my life offering me a world of insight— if I was willing to examine it. Part of me wanted to dive in anticipation of the revelations that would help me. Another part of me didn't want to unlock anymore of the stress and sadness I'd been trying to escape. But of course, these could only be overcome with an honest look.

I plopped down on the sofa, kicked off my sandals, and picked up *The Illiad*. After trying again to read the book for the fourth time in three months, and stopping again on page ten, I was tempted to throw the book onto the coffee table in surrender. It was a classic I'd promised myself I'd read the year before just because it seemed like one of those things that everybody should read at least once. I wanted to step up my reading game with "ancient stuff" that I imagined I'd discuss with professors and intellectuals at parties and museum events.

But whenever I went to Barnes and Noble with the intention of picking up something by Homer or the great philosophers, I ended up with Edgar Allen Poe or H.G. Wells. I would delve into heady and strange reads like *The Fall of the House of Usher* and, when I was in a spooky mood, wanting to shut out the world and revel in the esoteric, I listened to plays on Radio Mystery Theater.

I put down the copy of the Iliad and reached out for another book— a copy of *The Island of Doctor Moreau*. I fingered the pages as I briefly considered reading it. Its theme examined the plight of created beings at the hands of a quack doctor masquerading as God. It seemed to be a reference to the relationship between God and humans, and this metaphor had always been intriguing to me. It was a little bit creepy, and just might satisfy my taste for something primal.

None of this material, however, felt right. I needed something with a more sensual touch. I peeled myself off the couch and eased over to the kitchenette for a cup of mint tea. I turned around and admired the beautifully designed interior of my bungalow.

I had dreams of creating serene, romantic, mind-altering spaces. I had always been sensitive to my surroundings— analyzing flooring while walking through office corridors, checking out exposed ceiling structures in restaurants while everybody else chomped on chicken legs and corn. I once went to an opera at the Kimmel Center and spent half the show avoiding the snoozes by sneaking into various performance areas to compare the designs.

The kitchenette in my bungalow was lit with the subtle glow of small accent lights mounted along a dark mangrove beam above the bar. These were the only lights I used at night, besides a few candles next to my bed for reading. Just above that beam, the roof began to slope downward over a breakfast nook. The nook looked out over a completely unobstructed view of the resort through a large picture window that was flanked by two massive columns.

I could see several trees standing like guards around the bungalows— some erect, others leaning in to whisper to passersby walking in the cool breeze. Lights flickered on and off as the seniors who occupied most of the bungalows around mine turned in for the night.

Small fires were burning on a few patios, and I was drawn in by the prospect of the kind of warmth that emanated from them. I decided to lounge by my own fire pit. As I grabbed my journal from the kitchen counter and walked across the limestone floor, the surface of the walls reflected a hypnotizing, bluish moonlight.

I sat down and watched the flames, still unable to believe that everything had come to this. I couldn't understand why I was so quick to skip town with Jack's money, or what that would eventually mean.

I had fought with every fiber of my being to leave home, realize my dream of becoming an architect, and start a life for myself from scratch. After six years of study I was sixty-thousand dollars in debt, had far less confidence than when I first began, and was having regular tension headaches and jaw pain from grinding my teeth in my sleep (whenever I actually *could* sleep). And there were still two more years of school to go. Considering everything else, this hiatus was like a medical prescription.

Upon closing my eyes I could almost feel the strong and capable arms wrapping themselves around me. "Security," I whispered with a smile. The thought of Officer Stevens seemed harmless enough and was a great distraction.

Admittedly, he reminded me a lot of my ex-boyfriend, a man who had a certain way of making me feel safe.

My ex was quiet and peaceful, even a little shy— for a six-foot-two, two-hundred plus pound man. I used to marvel at his tone of voice, even when we disagreed. He never raised it, but always spoke quietly and with the calmness I imagined a father should display with his young daughter.

I flipped open my journal to an old letter I'd written to him when the long distance nature of our relationship started to get to me.

"Kobina, you are the first man that I have been able to love. You are the first man I've been comfortable enough with to even begin releasing myself to. You are the first man I ever kissed, embraced— and yes, there is still much to explore in that regard.

"I work hard to make you happy. I constantly force myself to remain honest with you. I stretch myself to be a support for you when you have hard times. I always make efforts to let you know that I care about you, your family, your work, your dreams, your goals. I want to be a part of your life— a refreshing addition to it. I've given to you from the most precious parts of me. And I want to give you even more of myself, emotionally, intellectually, and spiritually.

"There are times when I have many things to say to you, about the hopes I have for our relationship and what I want from you. But I can't say them. The desires, the words just sit in the pit of my stomach, an upsetting, jumble of passions that can't be articulated faster than they manifest in my physical body.

"Please explain to me again why it is that you say you love me. Your mind is alive with activity that I never experience, and I can't help but believe that there are many things that you're keeping from me. Why won't you talk to me?"

Kobina and I met just before I moved away from Virginia for school in Philly. I was twenty-one, and he was ten years older. During a nine-month period, I only saw him four times in person when I visited home. Otherwise, we'd talk each night after classes, and I'd struggle to get him to say more than a few words about any given thing—except sex.

I flipped back a few pages to an entry I wrote a few days before that letter. It was more of a rant about a conversation with him that had totally ticked me off. It lasted no longer than ten minutes, and when he could see that his one-hundredth reference to my virginity wasn't pushing the buttons he hoped it would, he was done talking.

"So, Kobina, how have you been?"

"Good, good."

"You didn't have classes today, right. Did you have a chance to visit the shop and check out that new camera?"

"No, Jane. I got some rest. I'm working tonight, so you know..."

"I checked out that PBS documentary about the war in Sierra Leone that you told me about. It was strange what they did with the camera angles, like you said."

"Ah… yes."

"But, overall they told a good story. Much of it seemed to come from the perspective of the people in the middle of the conflict— not so much just the filmmaker's take on things. I liked it. I'm glad you mentioned it."

"Yah, Jane… It was a good one…"

I shifted gears. Maybe that was too heavy of a subject.

"So, I had to turn in that wood framing project today."

"… okaaay."

"I think I did an okay job, even though I had trouble with the trusses in the end. There's always so much to get done, I feel really rushed all the time. How 'bout you? Did you brainstorm any new ideas for your documentary project?"

"No… not yet."

"How about your cousin, Kwesi? Has he been on any more big auditions?

"Nothing since *Tears of the Sun*. Everything else is small time, you know."

"Well, nothing wrong with small beginnings. Everybody has to start somewhere. You know, I was listening to the radio today and heard about an indie film festival that's going to be happening this summer. Up and coming filmmakers from all over the world are supposed to be there and they'll have like a meet-and-greet for film students. There's gonna be a panel discussion about documentaries made in parts of the world that are rarely portrayed in a positive light. Seems like something that could be really cool for us to go to."

"Yah, Jane… that sounds good."

"I know. I don't think we could pack the weekend with more than one big event. I'd like to have a chance to show you around, though. I know you said you've been through Philly but never really had a chance to stay. I'm getting to know so much of the city as part of my studies, but I've only seen a little nightlife. Maybe we can check out Cuba Libre, this Cuban restaurant I've been hearing a lot of good things about. They have salsa dancing shows on Saturday nights."

"… I can think of one thing that would be better than a festival or outing."

I was dreading what he would say next.

"Oh, really?"

"It would be your best birthday gift…"

He said that like an Ice Cream man offering a child a Push-Up popsicle.

"… how long you gonna make me wait to pop that cherry?"

Even though it appeared that he had the means to easily do so, I never asked him to come see me. He knew I was a virgin, and I knew I wasn't ready to have sex with him. I wanted the chance to get to know him better, and my Christian upbringing still had enough of a hold on me to make me want to wait for marriage. In-person meetings would only be inviting temptation.

I read the last line of that recorded conversation in my journal and then glanced over the thoughts I wrote just beneath it:

"YOU IDIOT! WHAT ELSE DID YOU EXPECT?!"

Looking into the fire, I blurted out to myself, "Why the heck did you invest so much in this guy?"

Back then, I hadn't realized that it would have been perfectly fine to just talk with him here and there, slowly getting to know him before committing to a "relationship" with all the burdensome expectations. In my mind, there was no place for casual dating in a Christian woman's life. There had to be some commitment from the get go.

"I didn't even know I had a choice." I said out loud.

I looked at the bungalow to my left and saw one of the guests release a slat in his blinds.

"All these people think I'm nuts." I said, closing my journal and leaning back to think more deeply.

It's unbelievable now, but there was once a point in our relationship when I was deluded into believing that we had something special, that I meant something to Kobina, and that the absence that made my heart grow fonder would culminate in some wonderful emotional adventure with him whenever we were together.

That one redeeming quality— his relative tenderness— made me dream up an entire relationship full of sharing and growing together. I wasn't thinking of marriage or even several years into the future. But I wanted to make our relationship count. He was, after all, my first official boyfriend.

However, the reality was, he had no interest in sharing anything with me other than sex. The distance later proved to be a convenient setup that kept one person in particular off his trail— his estranged wife.

Yep. His wife.

I had no idea he was married and didn't find out until two years after I broke up with him.

Call me loyal or stupid, but I never wanted to be that person who totally threw my ex away after breaking up with him. So, yes, we still talked from time to time. I'd stopped by to see him during a visit home one Christmas. His roommate and a friend were there.

The meeting was civil, and I didn't plan on staying for more than ten minutes or so. I glanced at him and commented on how he'd lost weight. It wasn't much, but just enough to make him look leaner.

He beamed with pride over the fact that he'd been working out. He rushed to his room, snatched his citizenship papers, and showed me the picture of himself attached to the top sheet. He was asking me to compare his current physique to what he looked like when he first moved to the U.S. from Ghana.

Immediately after looking at the photo, I glanced upward and saw his marital status, boldly printed directly above it.

"Married?!" I said, livid.

"So that's what the boring dinners cooped up in this apartment were about, huh? And you sitting all nervous at the edge of the very top row in the movie theater. You were scared you were going to get caught!"

He latched onto my arm and tried to get me to calm down so we could *"talk about this ting without gettin' all pissed off."*

There was nothing to talk about.

I wasn't going to waste my energy going off over a chapter in my life that was already closed. And, if I'm honest, I'll admit that I kind of always thought that there might have been another woman. What I didn't count on was that the other woman was me.

10

The sound of crackling firewood brought me back to the present. My energy was renewed after releasing some lingering emotional baggage from Kobina, and I wanted to go dancing.

I took a shower and slipped into a cute, lilac dress along with my new, nude-colored, wrap sandals with thick silky straps and Lucite heels. A thin gold chain and bracelet with some tinted lip gloss topped off the look, and I headed for the door.

Before I could make it out, though, my cell phone rang… again. I finally decided to pick it up.

"You couldn't pick up the phone and tell me you weren't coming back?"

"Jack, I told you I needed time and space to just clear my head."

"Email, Jane?"

"I can't do this right now." Tears were welling up in my eyes all of a sudden, and I was not trying to get emotional, puff up my eyelids, and spoil my impending fun.

"I told you I was keeping my promise, so I'm not trying to be all up in your space. But you don't feel even a lil' bit obligated to give me some idea of what's going on? Just gon' hop on a plane and send me a email, huh?"

I didn't have anything to say.

"I'm here, Jane. I'm here. But I'ma let you do your thing. And when you get ready to call me, when your *'head is clear'* and all that... you can call me."

***

The *Slip Away* was an old ship repurposed as a nightclub by some local Bermudian entrepreneurs. It docked at an inlet known for attracting travelers with shopping, hip international restaurants and late night parties. Each night, it traveled a few miles up and down the western edge of Somerset Village. Live bands played and strong-stomached club-hoppers attempted to dance the night away without sliding off the deck. Fortunately, the constant motion kept most people from drinking too much, which made for a peacefully festive atmosphere.

I made it to the dock just in time for the midnight sail. As I headed for the top deck, I began to feel a little nervous and out of my element. I couldn't loosen up with or shield myself behind a group of girlfriends.

And it wasn't easy to find my niche in this crowd— a mixture of noisy businessmen shouting what sounded like Portuguese, British vacationers discussing politics, a few middle-aged couples sprinkled here and there having drinks.

The New Year had begun and there were only a few lingering twenty-somethings who hadn't already had to rush back to classes or work.

I was reminded of my academic hub at school, the architecture studio, where I felt just as out of place as I seemed on this yacht. As the only black woman and someone who was several years older than the average roommate or student in my classes, I felt like a foreigner at school.

While many students were okay with resting in sleeping bags under their desks during all-nighters, I preferred to work alone in the privacy and warmth of my apartment. There, I could blast Anita Baker, Sade, or Mary J. Blige on my stereo and not have it interrupted with *I Don't Want to Be* by Gavin DeGraw. I could turn the lights down and burn some candles if the lighting became too harsh and annoying. I could stop and soak in a bubble bath if the thought of all the debt I was accumulating started to eat at me. I'd forego the old, hard-edged drafting tables, cold vinyl floors and metal chairs in favor of my cushy couch with the slipcover I made from scraps of interesting found fabrics. I could set the mood that my creativity needed to flow.

The scene on the boat reminded me how apprehensive I was about returning to an environment where I felt so out of place.

Just as I was becoming disappointed that the ship had begun sailing, eliminating the option of leaving, I heard the familiar sound of R&B music. No more of that pop junk that was played ad nauseam on radio stations back home. The mellow scene quickly morphed into a vibrant show of lively, cultured, adults enjoying their world. I was finally ready to dance.

Going dancing in different parts of the world is funny. The previous year, during my study abroad in East Africa, I and my comrades were amused to find clubs playing a mix of American pop songs from the early nineties as if they were current hits. Then there I was in a club in Bermuda with a bunch of middle-aged white people expecting to hear Calypso and reggae, but vibing to smooth R&B instead. I was pleasantly surprised to find that travel can be hazardous to one's assumptions.

On the dance floor, I found a few younger people who were good dancers and happened to be from the States. Christopher Ortiz, in particular, was a half Black, half Puerto Rican New York native. He was a thirty-year-old freelance writer who did most of his work for a minority run community newspaper in Brooklyn.

Through song after song, I channeled the spirit of my mother in her clubbing days before she dedicated her life to the Lord. I was like a young Yvonne James, rolling my shoulders, tossing my hair, and intuitively catching the beat.

I remembered her talking about how she used to dance so long and so hard she'd be dripping with sweat when it was time to leave. At the family reunion parties, I watched her carefully. Her technique was never over the top. She reached for the sky with poise and her serpentine hip rolls were the most graceful.

As Chris synced his movement with mine, I saw us in a mirror across the room and thought we looked good together. He was nice and tall. I was about six feet tall in my heels, so I didn't feel awkward next to him. He had thick, dark dreads, full eyebrows, and a mustache and goatee— all well-maintained and looking nice against his light skin. We were a cute combo.

Chaka Khan's *Ain't Nobody* faded into Milestone's *Sweet November,* which I had been jamming to several times a day for a month back home. I decided to stay on the dance floor for this one last song.

After that, when the DJ cranked up *All Nite* by Janet Jackson, I knew I couldn't take anymore.

"Hey, you're a great dancer." I said as we headed to the bar.

"Thanks. You're not too bad yourself." He pulled out a chair for me and we both sat down.

"Must come naturally. Kind of like your walk. Even that's sort of like a dance. You got that subtle sway." He smiled. "But let me not flirt too hard. What are you drinking?"

"Nothing fancy. Just ginger ale and water for me." I said handing the bartender my money before Chris had a chance to pay for it.

I never drank alcohol when I was out alone. I wanted to be as alert and in control of my surroundings as possible.

After the boat docked again we took a stroll down the boardwalk and talked about life in our respective towns.

"Did you say you're from Philadelphia?"

"I go to school there, but I'm originally from Virginia."

"That's kind of a long way from home. Think you'll go back there after you graduate?"

"Probably not. The vibe in Philly is better suited for me. Plus there's a greater chance of finding work in a more creative field."

"Well that's interesting that you've only been there a little while, because I can only hear a little bit of an accent. I can tell you're not from Philly, but your accent fades in and out."

"I'm always surprised when people say I have an accent, even a little bit of one. I guess you never notice what's so familiar to you. So what first got you interested in writing?"

"I first started writing when investors started buying up property in my old neighborhood." Chris said. "I would talk to my neighbors and my friends' parents who were concerned about their expenses going through the roof as stuff started changing. I wanted to record their perspectives on life in that neighborhood before it was all gentrified."

Wow. Another community-conscious man. It seemed that even though architectural study was presenting an unexpected challenge for me, the effortless connections that I was making might still lead me to my dream.

As he talked about the city planners, real estate brokers and architects that he met during his research, I thought about some of the discussions I'd participated in during the previous semester.

"It's interesting that you're studying architecture." Chris said. "Maybe you can help me understand something. I don't always get the thought process of some of the designers, you know. Do they try to engage with the public in more meaningful ways and then take what they learn back to the developers and say, 'look, these are the real needs in this community. I think we should design with this or that in mind?' I mean, where are the architects with more of a community mindset?"

"Well, they aren't the one's funding the projects." I said, echoing some of Jack's sentiments. "Those would be the developers, who are usually only interested in the income potential. Unfortunately, many architects don't consider community to be their area of concern."

He looked at me with a scrunched brow.

"One thing I'm learning in architectural training is just how little contact many architects have with the actual human beings who eventually inhabit their buildings. So many architects never meet those people on a regular basis, see how they live, hear their perspectives on how they want to live. A lot of these guys just work in front of a computer in an office ten or more hours a day. And many of the ones who do more creative work could care less about community cohesion in places like old Harlem or Brooklyn."

He stopped at an overlook to listen closely as I continued.

"In school, we're encouraged to pursue ideals— high design. We read treatises written by twentieth century, white German guys who decided what architecture would and wouldn't be, how people should and shouldn't live. Our projects consist of museums and visitor centers and high-rise new media centers and more visitor centers. It's always in the clouds, rarely down on earth. You wouldn't believe how many builders complain that architects know nothing about construction— it's because a lot of them spent so much time in school learning how to dream and how to think through an idea rather than learning how to get something built. The internship is supposed to teach us the practical stuff, but once you're in somebody's office, they just want you to work. They're not always interested in teaching at that point."

Chris asked, "So, you spend all this time in school developing ideals, not learning how to interact with real people on real projects? Then you graduate and have to find a way to teach yourself how stuff works in the real world. Isn't that line of work supposed to be like a service to humanity?"

"Depends on how the individual architect sees it. A lot of people simply consider it an art form, for art's sake. Last semester in a class discussion I asked, *'how do we begin our careers with a mindset of service to the communities around us?'* You know, I was getting at how to make design more relevant and useful for regular people. The professor flat out said, *'the architect's one and only obligation is to art, nothing else.'* "

"But that's so shallow and impractical it doesn't even make sense." Chris said. "I thought architecture was the fusion of beauty and function. What is it?" He snapped his fingers and searched for the words. "Form follows function, right? It starts with a purpose. Art with no goal to improve the human condition is not art. I have an aunt who's an interior designer, so I know a lil' bit."

"I'm afraid, too often, form follows ego. I don't know, maybe it's my school's curriculum in particular, but bootstrap theory seems to be very central to high design thought. It permeates everything from the academic prep, to licensure, and the work itself. Serving humanity or *helping people* is not often at the top of the list of priorities."

He looked out at a passing ship and said, "Well, that explains a lot. So why would you want to stick with that major, considering the apparent ethical conflict."

"Every profession has its ethical conflicts. And there are firms out there doing good work. I love the creative process and I've wanted to be nothing but an architect since I was a kid. I'll find a way to make it work. There's a way."

I looked at my watch and decided to call it a night.

"Well, Chris, I can't say I have to be in bed by a certain time, but if I don't head back soon, I'm gonna pass out. It was really nice meeting you. Maybe I'll see you out and about again before we go home."

"Why not make it a guarantee?" he said as I turned to leave.

I took a breath and slowly turned toward him. We were getting along so well that I'd figured a request for a date, or at least a casual meetup was inevitable. I had enjoyed his company and didn't want to reject the notion of seeing him again so quickly. But I'd promised myself that I wouldn't get entangled. I was determined to focus my attention internally.

"Uh, what do you mean?" I asked, unable to pull together the guts to say no.

"Why don't you just give me your number," he said with a reassuring smile, "and I'll call in the morning for breakfast, maybe."

"Did you just call me baby?"

"What? No, I said *'maybe'*... breakfast... You know, unless there's something else you gotta do."

"Oh."

I shrugged and fumbled around in my purse for the smallest piece of paper I could find then wrote my number on half a chewing gum wrapper. When I got back to my room the phone started ringing before I could get both my shoes off. I smiled and picked up.

"I hope I'm not bothering you."

"It's no problem." I said. "I was pleasantly surprised that you didn't lose my number."

Actually I'd left that one up to God. I'd figured if Chris lost the paper, it wasn't meant to be. But if he didn't, it was. Simple solution.

"I put it in my phone during the cab ride. Why didn't you just put my number in your phone?" he asked.

"Oh, I forgot my phone at my place."

I couldn't give him some weird, drawn out explanation of why I was trying to keep him at a distance but didn't want to just give him the cold shoulder.

"Hey, I won't take up too much of your time. I just wanted to tell you about this spot I found where we can have a nice breakfast, if you're interested."

"I might be game. What kind of food is it?"

"It's Jack Molloy's in Somerset, about a mile from the Slip Away dock. It has an Irish theme and the food is pretty similar to what you may be used to. Really good portions and all that. They hook you up. You know the area I'm talking about?"

I was able to quickly spot it on my tourist map as he was talking.

"Yep." I said.

"Wanna meet me at ten?"

"That'll work. Ten's cool."

We simultaneously said "Good night," laughed a little, and hung up the phone.

I turned off the TV and blew out the candle next to my bed. With my head finally on my pillow, I stopped to listen to the wave song outside my window. I closed my eyes and pictured the water washing gently against the shore. It wasn't long before the image of crystal waves melted into a dream, one that I had many times before.

***

Southern superstition says that if you dream of a dead loved one, it means you or someone close to you will soon die. Thankfully that had never happened, and I'd gotten over that fear after having this recurring dream for years with no such outcome. But I still had the eerie feeling that the appearance of my dead Grandma Sadie in this dream was more than wishful thinking or memories.

In the dream, I was at a reunion of my mother's family. Music was playing, children were riding around on rented ponies. I could even smell the charcoal from my Uncle Ronnie's grill. Everything was set in the present except that my Grandma Sadie sat across the yard with my mother and three aunts. She was in a wheelchair and looked confused, as she had been in the days shortly before her death.

As I approached her, she slowly began to raise her head from a low and tilted position. Her eyes began to squint and sparkle as I drew closer. In a very clear and deliberate manner she greeted me the way she always had, "Janie Boo." As if she'd been waiting all along to see me, she reached for my hand and gestured for me to lean in as she whispered something incoherent into my ear.

Then she reached into her pocket and pulled out a lush green plant. Handing it to me, her last words to me were clear, but I always woke up without the ability to remember them. This time was no different.

Awakened from the dream, I quickly turned on a light and wrote a note to document it in my dream journal. The rest of the night was quiet.

11

In the morning, my alarm clock startled me so bad that I fell out of the bed and onto the floor. I hadn't used the clock since exams, so I was no longer accustomed to its relentless chime. I was thankful for the pile of pajamas next to my bed that cushioned my fall. I'd wiggled out of them while sleeping, and I had to look at them for several moments before I could vaguely recall taking them off.

During my second year in Philly, as all-night homework sessions and erratic sleep became the norm, I developed a very strange habit. Besides the tooth-grinding, I started doing things in my sleep that I would barely remember after waking up. I'd have entire conversations with friends in the middle of the night and have to ask the next day what we talked about. Most notably, though, I undressed.

I didn't know if it was in response to a temperature spike, or the need to simply feel unencumbered, but it always gave me the weirdest feeling. I'd take my pajamas off in my sleep and be shocked to find them next to the bed in the morning.

Soon it became a regular thing, and I even became comfortable with the idea of being free from clothing during the day, too. That kind of freedom was a large part of the reason I decided to get my own place. It was a simple pleasure at a time of immense stress.

I was hardly faded by my tumble out of bed. I remembered the good time I'd had with Chris the night before, and I looked forward to meeting him for breakfast. After opening the shades to let in the morning light, I got dressed and rode my rented scooter to Jack Malloy's.

I arrived to a radiant view of relaxed vacationers having breakfast, drinking coffee and leaning over the patio railing looking for dolphins in the distant water. I found a table near the entrance where I thought it wouldn't be hard for Chris to find me, sat down and waited. It was five 'til ten o'clock, so I ordered us coffee and browsed the menu in the meantime.

After a few more minutes, I considered sending him a text to let him know where I was sitting. But I decided to give him more time.

"Jack wouldn't have been late."

That was beside the point. This was a vacation. I didn't have anywhere else to go.

At 10:20, Chris arrived and eagerly sat down beside me.

"Good! You already got us coffee."

I was slightly irritated by the lack of apology for his lateness, but I shrugged it off and turned to say hello. His red, squinty eyes, sluggish demeanor, and the thick smell of marijuana were immediately noticeable.

I shoved his coffee over to him and said, "Yeah, looks like you could use it."

At that moment my omelet and white pudding arrived, piping hot, and the server jotted down Chris's order. Conversation was scant and I just glared at him between bites and sips of orange juice. He mumbled about some article he wrote for an online magazine about the legalization of marijuana, or *"the liberation of herb"*, as he referred to it.

"See, when we liberate herb," he said, "we liberate ourselves. From the illusion of propriety. I mean, alcohol is legal anyway, right? And tobacco, now that's the plague right there, but it's legal, right? This so-called war on drugs just feeds the beast of the prison industrial complex. Everybody should see this… it's a no brainer!"

I started cutting my next portion of omelet when I heard him quietly mutter "Oh, damn."

I looked up and saw him making the sorriest attempt to conceal a bag of weed that fell out of his pocket and onto the patio floor. He shuffled his feet out from under the table, kicking the bag underneath it with his foot. He kept his arms close to his side, as if trying to keep a low profile, and quickly looked back and forth over both shoulders.

I held back an onslaught of insults as the server arrived with his bacon and eggs, sunny side up.

He stared at the eggs, seemingly with suspicion, and finally began to eat. I did my very best to ignore him for the rest of our time there. As I polished off my white pudding and prepared to leave, I was again distracted by his noise-making. I looked up and was stunned to see Chris fast asleep and beginning to snore.

Finally, I figured a little going off was long overdue. So, I stood up, shoved his nodding head into his plate and screamed, "Wake up, jackass!!"

"Ay, wus wrong wit' you?" he slurred, picking eggs from his goatee.

As I stormed off, I remembered that I hadn't yet paid my own bill, and I didn't care.

***

"Katrina!" I yelled. "Katrina, pick up your phone, girl! I got another one for you."

My phone indicated an incoming call as I was recording this message. I hit the answer button knowing it would be my best girlfriend from Virginia calling back.

"What's up, girl? How you been?" I said.

She answered in her usual, breezy, sing-songy way. "I'm good, Ladybug. How's Ber-mu-da? I know you havin' a good time. I hope you relaxin' some for me!"

"It's wonderful. It's so beautiful, I don't wanna leave." I said in an intentionally dry and rushed voice as I released my hair from a loose ponytail and began unfastening my dress.

"Let me tell you about this fool I just had breakfast with, then we can get to the good stuff."

She laughed. "Girl, the men are working your nerves already?"

"I can't tell you why I expected anything different." I said.

I kicked off my sandals, slipped out of the dress, jumped onto the couch and waited to feel some relief from the shedding of a little extra weight. Then I told her about my dancing and breakfast with Chris.

"That is RI-DI-CU-LOUS. You mean to tell me he showed up high, like that?!"

"High as a kite." I assured her as I began picking at my ears to remove my hoops. "It's a shame because, as smart as he is, I hope he don't fry all his brain cells with that mess. Half of the things he mumbled, I couldn't even understand."

"Oh my God! What in the world is wrong with him? I'ma call this one 'Smoke.' How you gon' show up high, all willy-nilly like that? You can't even wait 'til later in the day? You already lit up at TEN A.M.?! Maybe it's a Caribbean thing."

"I wouldn't say that." I said as I rotated my bra around in order to undo the clasp. "Technically, this isn't the Caribbean. Plus, dude is American. He's just a weedhead."

Still feeling downright stifled, I opened the kitchen and living room windows and then quickly removed my underwear. I remembered to close the blinds next, but as I reached for the lever, an amazing breeze came through the window along with the refreshing smell of the bay. I didn't think I could be seen since a line of trees concealed the walkway in front of my windows. I shut my eyes and took in the breeze. When I opened them, there was Ali walking toward my door.

"Oh my God!" I yelled while lunging toward the floor. After sliding into a hiding space behind the kitchen island, I peeked above it and saw him raising his hand to knock.

"What is it, girl? Are you okay?" Katrina asked.

"Somebody at the door!"

"Oh." she said, sounding confused. "Don't answer it. It might be Jack!"

"Get out a here, girl! No, it's this guy." I said.

"The one from this morning? Girl, open that door and hit him upside the head with a frying pan! Kick 'im in the nuts!"

"No, not that guy. It's this security guard. I met him last night. Kept getting in my space while I was trying to relax on the beach. Girl, he's fine as I don't know what, though. Looks like Shaka Zulu with a few extra pounds of muscle."

"I thought you met Smoke last night."

"I did."

"So you met Smoke AND Shaka last night?"

"Yes, Katrina."

"Two men in one night? And you been there three days? You done got a little wild in Philly, Jane. You sure Jack didn't turn ya out? What else do I need to know?"

"Puh-lease!"

"So, why you don't want to open the door?"

Still peeking over the countertop, I paused then whispered, "Because I don't have any clothes on."

"Hold up." Katrina's voice lowered and took on a serious and suspicious tone. "You ain't got no clothes on? You on the phone wit' me wit' no clothes on?"

"I just got undressed when I came in." I tried to explain.

"And you still haven't found anything else to put on YET? Girl, why are you walking around the place with no clothes on?"

"Sshh! I gotta whisper real low until he walks away." I said. "He might be able to hear me through the windows."

"He ain't gon' hear me, though. You walking around naked with your windows open, too?!" Katrina yelled.

"Look," I said, "I paid for this bungalow. It's mine for now. And if I don't want to wear a stitch, I'm not wearin' a stitch."

"OKAY!" she said, laughing. "I'll wait. But I'm going to have to tell Patricia we got to keep an eye on you. You getting out of hand."

"Girl, chill out."

"Do you at least got your drawers on?" she asked.

When I didn't answer, she said, "Hmph," and kept waiting.

Finally, Ali stopped knocking and walked away. I ran into the bedroom, grabbed my robe, returned to close the blinds, and let the robe fall to the floor again. After Katrina finally stopped laughing at me we resumed our conversation, and she took me on a trip down memory lane.

"You know what I was just thinking about the other day?"

"What?" I asked.

"That time we snuck into the Westin at the ocean front to see the rooftop pool! You remember those water guns we hid under our shirts?"

"Yep! That couple in the atrium kept looking up trying to figure out where the water was coming from. Then the lady had the nerve to put up an umbrella!"

"I know," Katrina laughed. "And you remember when you liked that guy, Jonathan, one of them Kappa pledges, but was too scared to talk to him. So acting stupid one night, we played knick-knock at his door. He came in the hallway in his robe like, *'what the hell'*!"

Katrina and I laughed about that for a good while, then she continued.

"I saw Big Buff the other day, too! He still looks the same, swole as ever. He doesn't have his cornrows anymore, though. I spoke and almost called him Big Buff, like we used to call him. But then I remembered his name and was like, *'Heeeey Gino'*."

"Yeah, girl!" I said. "I miss goofing off with you all like that. Hopping in the car at midnight for a chicken run. Y'all called my car a clown because whenever we pulled up, like twelve of us would come piling out."

"I KNOW! Those were the days. But you always were scared of men, Jane."

"What are you talking about? I interacted with guys all the time."

"Yeah but you were always scared to approach the ones you really liked. Wouldn't even say hello to them."

"He who findeth a wife findeth a good thing, Katrina."

"Yeah, Jane, but that don't mean you can't EVER speak up and show some interest. Don't try to hide behind that. I respect the church and all, but I'm not gon' let no preacher tell me I can't go after the man I want! Oh, and remember when we went with you to see Maxwell in *Jesus Christ Super Star*?"

I closed my eyes and dropped my head. Not this again. I didn't want to be reminded of the fact that she and my other two best friends back home had witnessed me carry on in one of the strangest relationships I'd ever experienced. I would never hear the end of it. This one almost topped even Jack.

"Where did you meet him, again?" Katrina asked.

"We knew each other in elementary school." I said. "We were in first, second, and third grade together. We played boyfriend and girlfriend for like two weeks once. I shared him with this girl named Yolanda James, cuz he got on my nerves but I still wanted to be his girlfriend. Yo was supposed to help take the edge off. Even as kids we had this weird poly thing going."

I laughed to myself and stopped for a moment to ponder how that setup may have contributed to the weird thing that became my relationship with Maxwell later on.

"Anyway, that's how it started. We lost touch after elementary school then ran into each other after, like, ten years."

"Ooooh. Well, could you tell then that he was… ummm… effeminate?"

"Not so much as kids. But later on, yeah. And girl, you can say it. It was clear that he was not straight once we got a little older."

"Then how in the WORLD did y'all take such an interest in each other?" she asked.

"Well when we met up again, we just connected. There was a natural chemistry and we had a lot in common. One time he told me about this party he went to where he met this girl that he was attracted to. The way he described it, it sounded to me like a romantic attraction— not an *'I'd kill to have those heels she was wearing'* kind of attraction. He definitely was into men, but whether or not he was into women— the jury was still out on that. We started hanging out all the time, and just really enjoyed each other's company."

"Oh! So he's bi?" Katrina said.

"I think so. He's never said that. But it's crazy with bisexuals. It's like, LGBT people get crap all the time from people who say, *'I just don't understand how they can be like that. They're confused.'* Then some gay people turn around and do the same thing to bisexuals saying, *'They're just greedy. They can't figure out what they want. I don't get them.'* I guess everybody's looking for somebody to put down.

"Anyway, I think if he is bisexual, he wasn't ready to admit it then because he was already alienated enough.

We had this genuine chemistry. The connection was undeniable from the beginning. But he wasn't at peace with who he was, I don't think. He was struggling with wanting to stay in the church and not being able to change who he felt he really was.

"His mom was always putting him down, his church friends had him in some kind of homo-therapy, trying to cure him. It seemed like I came around at a time when he was more than happy to have a shield from all of those people scrutinizing him."

Katrina jumped in, "Oh, so you think he was using you to put up a front? You were his beard?"

"I don't think that was his intention, but meeting me, having me over for dinner, having me stop by on Saturday nights, and knowing we were spending so much time together definitely seemed to make his mom and church friends happy. If he was having a genuine attraction to and a good relationship with a girl, they figured God was healing him or something." I said.

"And that meant they put less pressure on him." Katrina said.

"Maybe… I guess. It all seemed too convenient."

For the umpteenth time, Katrina got ready to ask the question I hoped she'd avoid. I guess she never could wrap her mind around what Maxwell did when things really peaked between us. Neither could I, really. I decided to cut her off at the pass.

"No, I never considered marrying him! I couldn't even call him a legitimate boyfriend. He was living with a guy half the time that we were… together. And how the heck can you take a guy seriously who asks if you'd marry him but only under the condition that the two of you keep an extra man around to take turns having sex with, because he can't stand the thought of having sex with a woman and he knows that you've both got to be satisfied somehow?!"

Katrina erupted with laughter. "Oooh, girl! That mess is TOO much! TOO much! How do you become romantically involved with a woman, but you get turned off by the thought of having sex with women?"

"One time he said something like, *'I think a man corrupts a woman when he has sex with her.'* He used to say, *'So many men are just not yet as evolved as women. They just dumb you guys down."*

"So, so strange... He asked you like three times." Katrina added.

"It wasn't a proposal. It was more like: *'Jane, do you think you could see yourself as my wife'* or *'Jane, would you marry me once we're older and ready to settle down'* or *'Jane, could you be married to someone you don't have sex with?'* Anyway, maybe it wasn't attraction at all. Maybe for him it was fascination... like getting a new toy or playing with a doll."

"Humph, that's how it is even with some straight men! That's just crazy, being married but not having sex?" Katrina ranted.

"It's not as uncommon as you think." I said.

Katrina continued, "Why would he do that stuff when he knew he couldn't live up to it. He can't be no woman's husband."

"Selfishness? I don't know. He was in fantasy land. He *lived* in fantasy land— it was overwhelming."

"He was in fantasy land... with you." Katrina paused for what sounded like a drink then laughed.

"Well, girl, I'd love to work your nerves a lil' more with all our past shenanigans, but I gotta get back to these collection calls. You know these fools watch everything we do around here. If I get back to my cube a minute late, the supervisor is already standing there. But you enjoy yourself! Have a dance or two for me! Oh… and put some clothes on and go check on Shaka!"

I promised to give her a call once I was back in Philly.

I sat in the comfortable cross breeze in the living room and flipped through my journal looking for the entries I wrote during my time with Maxwell. Anger and frustration over Chris were beginning to put me into a funk that was briefly made worse from my disappointment in finding that I hadn't written much about Maxwell. I was really hoping to pick through my thoughts from that time and through some good memories.

Then I realized that the lack of a stream of entries documenting that experience could mean only one thing. I was happy then. And what did that mean for my life now if a relationship like the one I had with Maxwell, despite all its oddness, made me happy?

I only wrote profusely in my journal when I was in emotional distress, which seemed to be more often than not in my teen years. If my parents had yet another fight and I was frustrated with my mom's inability to leave a bad situation, I wrote reams. If I was upset about being called a nun by some raggedy high school junior looking for a quick piece, ten pages would flow easily from my fingertips. If I was bursting with feelings for a man that I didn't feel good enough to approach and had no other way to express them, I scribbled for hours at a time.

Journaling separated me from my feelings a little and gave me the distance I needed to analyze them. But there was nothing much about my relationship with Maxwell that required analyzing, because it had been so effortless. The one entry that explained it was this:

"Maxwell is the most communicative man I've ever spent time with. I have never been able to feel such a depth of love and sincerity from a guy. When he gives me a hug, I feel like some part of my spirit has been fed. He doesn't leave ten inches between us, tap me on the back and rush away. It's not like those phony church hugs everybody gives each other when the pastor forces neighbors to acknowledge each other but everybody's scared of touching people's intimate parts. And there's no groping.

"He's told me he loves me many times and I know he means it. He holds my hand in silence and I can feel that love without either of us having to say a word. I can rest in it without any anxiety or sense of obligation.

"He can be a lot to handle with all of his dreaming, and emotion, and conflicts, and probing questions. I know he's just trying to bring the best out of me and that he's actively working on himself. But he's hyper, and never knows when to chill. He wants to run around all hours of the day and night and never wants me to go home. He can be a real snob and really rude to people. He stopped by Katrina's with me once and mentioned how much he hated the design of her apartment because it was outdated. Who the heck cares!

"He's an emotional wreck. Last night, on the interstate, we drove past a trail of blood from some kind of road kill. He burst out crying uncontrollably— as he has done several times before— saying, "I just hate to think that a living creature suffered for so long". I don't think he was actually referring to the animal.

"I don't want to see him suffer. I do love him. I want to hang out with him and keep letting him teach me about art, and rich people, and his business ideas, and meditation. As a Christian, I should also make the effort to show him genuine love and concern. I don't want to be like everyone else who just wants to shove him into a box. He fears that if he changes, he'll lose his creativity, that he'll no longer be who he fundamentally is, and I fear the same thing.

"Without the pressure to be sexually involved, I am literally satiated by a love that I've never imagined could be so palpable and soothing. But there is no way this could ever stand the test of time. Things that feel this good never do. My mom says we have an unhealthy soul tie that is a trick of the enemy, and that I should go on a fast with her to break it."

I knew that viewing this as a relationship with long-term potential would be completely foolish, and I eventually pulled away without looking back. I never even considered the possibility of a lasting, close friendship, not with all that stuff my mom was saying about tricks of the devil and catching a "spirit of homosexuality" from him. However, after that time with Maxwell, no encounter with a man, emotional or physical, ever came close to being so deeply satisfying— until Jack.

A huge part of me wanted to know if things had gotten any better for him since we parted four years ago. So, I decided to give him a call.

"Hi, Maxwell." I said after the beep, "We haven't talked in a while, so I just called to see what's up. Hope you've been doing well. Give me a call when you get this."

12

I've heard women compare their relationships to some strange things. Jessica once said being with her boyfriend was like raising a Rottweiler. She thought she had to keep him on a tight leash to "train" him, or he'd overpower her the first chance he got.

A lady in a grocery store checkout line once told me that marrying a man was like adopting a feral teenage boy. Ten years into their union, she still had to beg her husband to shower and remind him to flush the toilet after using it. I guess *his* training went awry.

Some people's marriages are like downright war. Whether it's a cold war with silence and hidden resentments or a hot war full of blows, it was still two people at odds and trying to win. This had been my preferred metaphor for my parents' marriage.

These metaphors served a purpose, I guess. They helped people to sum up their experiences in one quick illustration that gave them clear perspective on what was happening in their relationships.

I wanted to come up with a metaphor for my dating life. It had to be one that would get me psyched up about Devi's assignment and even make me laugh a little so I could get through it without getting depressed.

After my blast-from-the-past conversation with Katrina, a brief afternoon rain had begun to fall. This was the perfect opportunity to write, so I decided to pull out a fresh new notebook from my carry-on bag and start brainstorming.

Call it divine intervention or just perfect timing, but as I yanked my notebook out, an old, crumpled up ad for the UniverSoul Circus came tumbling out with it. I took one look at those dancers dressed in Technicolor tribal wear that looked like something from the engagement party scene in *Coming to America* and thought, *"Yep, that about sums it up"*.

My theme was set. I'd just take a quick cat nap and wake up refreshed and ready to write.

***

"WELLLLLLCOOOOME TO DAME FLUKE'S BEGUILING TOURING BIZARRIUM AND PANDEMONIUM SHOOOOOOOOOOW! The greatest escapade *YOU'LL* ever see!"

The deafening blare of those words reverberated all around me. Lights of all colors were flashing, bouncing off what looked like a hundred strobe lights swinging wildly from the ceiling of a circus tent.

Sisqo's *Thong Song* started playing, and the scene before me crystalized into a portrait of animals and performers preparing for the most mind-blowing of spectacles. The voice continued:

"First up! A loveable gang of adventuring nitwits who'll knock your socks off with their zaniness! A super-cool troupe of fun-loving fellas with tricks like the world has never seen! Watch 'em set themselves on fire and run over each other with motorcycles! They can do magic tricks— drunk or sober! And boy do they have moves that can kill! Give it up for Flimflam, Tookadoo, Sleezlebub, and Bop!"

A cloud of smoke exploded from the floor, and out of it scampered four hyped up chimpanzees wearing jeans, leather jackets, and sneakers. Flimflam stood in the center of them and struck a pose before breaking into a wild dance routine, complete with a provocative shirt ripping.

Tookadoo and Sleezlebub ran toward me with bouquets of roses that disappeared each time I tried to grab them but reappeared whenever I gave up. I had to smack the chimps away repeatedly to avoid being kissed and licked by them.

Finally, Bop sped onto the stage on a black motorcycle that skidded to a halt right in front of me. He hopped off, adjusted his diamond encrusted necklaces and watch, and pimp-walked over to me, screaming at the top of his lungs and beating his chest.

Just as the four of them gathered up for a juggling trick, I was approached by a cotton candy vendor.

"Cotton Candy, Baby? Premium sugar on a stick."

He licked his lips.

"No thanks!" I said, despising the suggestion.

He insisted, "Errybody need a lil' sugar. Hey, I'll give you my best price. Two hundred dollars."

"Two hundred dollars! You're crazy!"

"Hey, baby, this ain't yo' usual cotton candy. Ain't nobody but you can get that deal, cuz I like yo' style. Come on, this is the best thing smokin'!"

I waved my hand, motioning for him to go away. He left graciously, yelling into the crowd, "Cotton Candy! Sugar on a stick! As good as it gets!"

The MC continued in the booming voice, introducing the next act.

"Here comes Binky the Clown! He's cute, harmlessly dopey, and he's got that classic unassuming sweetness that just melts the ladies' hearts."

As the MC went on and on with the introduction, Binky dragged himself across the stage looking nothing like the loveable personality the MC described. He wore a large, green Afro, a frilly clown shirt with an oversized bowtie, a diaper, and huge clown shoes. But his disposition was dry and apathetic.

He started pulling junk out of his shirt pockets. He threw old tissue and candy wrappers here and there then walked quietly toward me with a balloon hanging from his mouth.

Standing there expressionless, he blew up the balloon into a long cylindrical form. He tied it to a string then tied the string around his waist so that the balloon flopped pitifully in front of his diaper. Without blinking, he put his hands on his hips and waited for the crowd to respond.

I was livid.

"Oh, give me a friggin' break!" I yelled, throwing my head back in irritation. "Where's this great show you keep talking about?!"

Binky quickly became just as upset and stood there with a big frown before throwing a kicking, screaming tantrum.

He had to be hauled off the stage by two ushers while the MC gave her remarks.

"Uh-ooooh! Looks like that mean lady didn't get Binky's joke!"

Spectators in the surrounding seats all gave me nasty looks. I rolled my eyes.

"And now, the most alluring, tantalizing, and unbelievable thing you never imagined you'd see! Watch Royal Chieftain Doctor Scamalot— our most magnificent ringmaster— turn this WILD, SNARLING, RAGING, UNCOUTH, UNSENSIBLE, UNBEEEEEARABLE BEAST into a pleasant, obedient, and yes, even effervescent, kitten."

A spotlight onstage grew ever brighter as the announcer stepped forward to reveal herself and to say her last, instigating words. When she emerged, I lost my breath upon seeing what I instinctively knew was an old, gray-haired version of me.

The audience applauded wildly. With eyes wide and entrancing, she pointed to me and screamed,

"TAKE IT AWAAAAAY, DOC!"

One second I was in the audience, and the next, I was right in the middle of the stage. I blinked in astonishment as Flimflam, Tookadoo, Sleezlebub, and Bop shackled my limbs to the floor. I looked down to find four golden brown paws where my hands and feet should have been. Then I looked back up and saw Scamalot motioning calmly toward the audience before he turned to me with a bow.

Panicking, roaring, raking my claws across the wooden stage, I tried to escape the shackles.

Scamalot reassured the audience, "Once she's fully in the clutches of my will she will fight no longer." He opened the door to the cage and turned toward me. I saw his raised whip just as I locked eyes with him.

He cracked the whip against the floor once… twice… three times. I could tell that he was alarmed to find that his movement had not triggered my reflexes or distracted me in any way.

I felt an unnatural strength well up within me, and I lunged forward with a frothy growl, breaking two of the chains as I came face to face with Scamalot.

My eyes suddenly popped open and looked around. Sweat dripped from my brow. I was back on my couch in my quiet bungalow, awake with no chains, no monkeys, and no cage.

***

I slowly pulled on a loose tank top over a sports bra and jeans, still disgusted by that Freudian twilight zone of a dream. There was a haze of melancholy around me that I hadn't felt in some years. I figured it was a mixture of fatigue, PMS, and spending too much time in my head. It wasn't overwhelming, and some activity or another, like doing my devotions, dancing, working, or working out, usually kept it in check.

Since looking within was what this trip was all about, though, I'd accept my feelings for what they were and allow them to lead me to whatever insight I needed.

I headed out for lunch, but had my agenda interrupted when Ali saw me step onto the boardwalk.

"Jane, right?" he asked. "I stopped by your bungalow earlier."

He seemed oddly cheerful. I kept walking, and tried to brush him off quickly so I could maintain my deep, contemplative mood.

"What did you want?" I asked, without looking in his direction.

"I just wanted to make sure you were doing okay. It was kind of odd seeing you out by the water like that."

I turned toward him finally and said,

"Yeah… I'm good."

He went on, "The neighbors, you know, they get concerned about strange stuff like that. One of 'em said he saw you outside last night, by your fire pit talking… but there was nobody there with you."

"Oh, come on!" I said, completely annoyed. "People spend their money and fly all the way out here to be on the BEACH and they think somebody's crazy for wanting to be near the water? And why are they poking their noses into my space, worrying about what I do in front of my fire pit?"

Ali laughed while I went on.

"I guess he was the one who told you my name too, huh? Probably gave you a copy of my boarding pass and photo ID."

"Nope, I found that all by myself." he said, still chuckling.

I pretended to be surprised and joked, "All by yourself, huh?"

He nodded as if he'd figured out a mystery.

"So you just came here for a little getaway?"

My phone rang as he was talking.

"I'm on vacation like everyone else here."

"And you came all the way from Philly by yourself? You have any family or friends here?"

I looked at my phone and saw that Maxwell was calling.

"No, I don't have any people here— wait a minute! How do you know I came from Philly?"

He grinned and admitted, "I actually did see a copy of your boarding pass. You must have left it at the reception desk by mistake, because they put it in your file. I was going give it back to you when I came—"

"Hello, Maxwell. How have you been?"

Ali waited.

"Well, I'm in Bermuda... Yeah, classes do start again soon."

I finally looked up to excuse myself from the conversation with Ali and to avoid letting him overhear anything too personal.

"Alright, I'll talk to you later." he mouthed with a happy grin.

I waved and then turned to find a place to sit while I caught up with Maxwell. The talk quickly progressed from pleasantries to more serious topics, including the end of our time together.

"I was never really sure what you thought about my performance in *Jesus Christ Superstar*." he said. "I'd hoped you would like it."

"It wasn't quite the type of entertainment I was used to, but I think you did a great job in your performance." I said.

The truth was, for a bunch of church girls who had never veered far from our Baptist and Pentecostal backgrounds, Jesus Christ Superstar was difficult for me and my friends to understand, at best. At worst it seemed blasphemous.

This was something that Maxwell could easily understand, being from a Pentecostal background himself. But I knew he wouldn't be satisfied with my answer. He wanted me to give a worthy analysis of the play and of him in the play. Unfortunately, I hadn't been enthralled enough to form much of an opinion, and I didn't have the guts to tell him that I just didn't like the play.

"Well, what did you think about the depiction of Judas?" he asked. "Were you intrigued by the degree of dimension applied to his character?"

"It was an interesting depiction, but seems like they used a touch of artistic license on that one."

"Is artistic license not proper to use in a play?"

"Sure, but the bible doesn't really describe Judas as a sympathetic character."

There it was, that religious shut-off valve that could stop the flow of thought midstream. I tried not to use it when talking to Maxwell, because he had always worked so hard to encourage me to broaden my perspectives. But the need to defend certain biblical certainties I believed in was still second nature for me.

"Riiight." he said slowly. He was as patient as he'd always been.

"What I was hoping for was more of a thoughtful opinion based on the actual content of the play. Not necessarily a review of scripture."

"Do you want me to say I liked the play, Maxwell?" I teased him a little.

"I don't want you to *lie* and say you liked it— oh, forget it, I'm just glad to hear from you."

"I'm glad to talk to you again, too. How's teaching going?" I said, relieved to be done with another probing.

"The private school environment is so much more nurturing. I can offer the students a lot more, you know. That month I spent in the public school system was hell. I wouldn't go back to that for anything. It's a total shit show compared to the way things are run when they're properly funded. Things are going well now. Our theater arts program is really taking off and I'm coaching several students privately for an upcoming opera intensive."

This was good news, however, something in his tone seemed to precede a *"but"*.

"Actually, just a couple days ago, I went to the French restaurant we went to that time I showed you around the VCU campus, back when I was in college. I hadn't been there since then… That was a really nice lunch."

I could hear his voice getting softer and a little sad.

"I was actually hoping you would like the play." he said quickly.

I wasn't sure how to respond. In the past, I had never wanted to be too blunt or to set myself at odds with him by disagreeing too often. I was afraid too much disagreement would disturb our connection. I was also so insecure that I never felt that my intelligence could quite match his, so I overanalyzed everything before I said it.

Once again, he was being vulnerable and attempting to invite me in, and I couldn't escape it easily.

"You know, Jane, I guess I'm pressing this because there was something about that story that was very integral to what I was experiencing at the time." He paused as if he was waiting for something. "I just wondered if you got it."

He waited again for me to respond.

"I really cared for you. I loved you." he said.

"I loved you too, Maxwell. I still do."

Though I couldn't stand being such a coward, silence overtook me. Then he began to quietly hum the chorus to Nelly Furtado's *I'm Like a Bird*.

He called out, *" 'IIIIIIII'm Like a Bi-i-iiiiiird'."*

Pausing again, his voice then went low one more time as he sang, " *'I don't know where my soul is. I don't know where my home is'.* Will you fly away again?"

I perked up in my chair. I had always thought he was referring to himself when he sang that song. Was he directing that question to me?

"I don't know what that means." I finally said.

"The part about flying away or about me loving you?" he asked.

I didn't respond.

"Well… if you still love me, I hope you're still praying for me."

"Why, what's going on?" I asked.

By his tone, I wondered if he was having a hard time with his students or colleagues or if his family was giving him trouble again. But it was much worse than that.

13

"My partner was murdered. A little over a year ago. We were leaving a club one night and some guys from Park Place starting taunting us. They were drunk. You know Park Place. I don't know why they haven't moved that club to a different neighborhood, but I guess they're waiting out the changes. You *know* that place is gentrifying."

My grandmother lived in Park Place, right down the street from the gay club that Maxwell used to frequent with Rob. After visiting her once, we had a good laugh over the look of surprised amusement that covered her face as she observed Maxwell. Then he told me all about the long-term urban plan for Park Place and this part of Norfolk, which he had researched extensively.

"Anyway, I ran my mouth for a minute and Rob yelled at me to get in the car. He just wanted to ignore them and leave— he was always the type to take the high road. One of the guys just would not leave him alone. I buckled my seatbelt, saw Rob get in, but then something was pulling him back out of the car. "

His voice got really quiet as he continued recalling events, painting a picture with words and tones in myriad colors the way he always did.

"He had his arm around Rob's neck when I got back out. Of course, the ignoramus would not have assumed that Rob was a martial artist. He flipped the guy over and punched him in the stomach. When the guy realized he was getting his ass kicked by a gay white guy he started screaming for his flunky to help him… and they both started kicking him.

"Jane, I did what I could, but there were *three* guys. You wouldn't believe the disgusting things they said. *'You might be gay, but you don't know prison gay, you faggot. I'd make you wanna turn straight if you had been in my cell!'* "

"Some people in the club heard what was going on and came out to help… I noticed them pouring out of the club. Then I turned back… to look at Rob, and saw one of the guys kick his head into the pavement… like he was a roach crawling across a floor. He was in a coma for a week."

"Oh… I… I'm so, so sorry."

I didn't know what else to say and didn't want to make matters worse by trying to talk through the silence too soon.

"… I can't imagine how hard things must be for you after that. "

"It's been a long, hard year," he said honestly.

"Has your family, your mother been much support?" I asked, hoping that things between him and his mom had returned to a good place, even if in the midst of a tragedy.

He laughed.

"No, I'm afraid not! And I thought Louise still had a tender heart under all that vitriol. No, she was actually more concerned that her colleagues on the school board or some of those saints would see the news reports that I was mentioned in. She was beginning to come around with me but was still in denial about us living together for so long."

Being reminded of the dynamic between Maxwell and his mother was just as heart-wrenching as the story of how Rob died. I had always remembered Louise be a beautiful, quiet, calm and confident woman. A woman who worked hard on behalf of children and served the church. As her son, Maxwell had a deep admiration for those qualities in her and was proud to have inherited her regal form, bright eyes, and strong yet graceful hands.

The closeness and warmth he'd shared with her as a boy had, when he was older, given way to violent arguing over his late night partying, visceral insults about is hairstyling choices and passive aggressive promises to "pray for his soul." Yes, I was sure he'd always love and admire her, but hatred always seemed to be just beneath the surface.

"When I told her," he went on, "The first thing she said was, *'I just knew running around like this would be your downfall eventually. Death becomes of it.'* "

I had to admit that something like this had always been my ultimate fear for Maxwell. I had heard too many preachers and church ladies talk about the *"consequences of the gay lifestyle"* and openly express disdain for the gay men with AIDS who *"deserved what they got"* for living in *"perversion"*. The same people who held their heads high as the ambassadors of truth and love to a dying world were the ones cheering in their hearts whenever something like this happened. They actually expressed more indignation over a person's sexual orientation than for the fact that he or she had been murdered or abused for it.

He must have sensed what I was thinking.

"Do you think God is punishing me?"

"Absolutely not!" I said immediately. "Don't even go there."

"He punished me long before now." he said.

"How?"

"Being gay is punishment enough."

He paused, and neither of us spoke. We both knew better than to interrupt the moment. I didn't try to correct or console him. He didn't need that.

"Anyway, I'm really glad to talk to you again. I'm glad you called. I considered calling you long before now, but I've been thinking of making a big move.

"Oh, really? Where?"

"I'm thinking of moving out west, San Francisco. I know it sounds really cliché. I considered Chicago, but I'm leaning toward some better job prospects in the school system in San Francisco. If I decide to take the plunge, I'll let you know… It was nice to hear from you Jane."

"It was good talking to you too, Maxwell. Please take care of yourself."

***

I was full of mixed emotions. I felt bad for losing touch with Maxwell. I also felt horrible for not loving him back as strongly as he had loved me, but then I wasn't sure that was something I could have controlled.

I cared deeply for him and I had truly been changed by all of the new experiences he introduced to me. But I had spent too much time with him out of a sense of obligation. I was a people pleaser, and I didn't know just how bad that could be until I reunited with Maxwell. I indulged him, partly out of an accommodating nature and my inability to say no or set boundaries. In the end, there was a part of me that just needed to move on. That part of me felt like I'd let him down when he needed someone most, and I wasn't so sure that wouldn't happen again.

14

One week had passed, and I hadn't written a thing. I'd pored over my old journals, dredging up a bunch of anger and self-pity along the way. I'd had lunch with a weedhead, mulled over the pathetic fact that my first official boyfriend had been someone else's husband, and picked off the scab of my relationship with Maxwell by refreshing my anxiety over disappointing him. And there was *still* Jack to consider.

"Where the heck is it?" I asked myself while getting dressed in front of the bedroom mirror.

"This must be what guys are seeing when they look at you. Is it in the eyes, the expression?"

I scanned my face looking for the invisible energetic stamp that I thought was definitely plastered somewhere. The one that labeled me unsuitable for a serious and authentic romantic relationship with an available, straight man. The one that must have said something like this:

JERK MAGNET. ALL WHO ARE DUMB, DISHONEST, STALKY, CRAZY, AND SIMPLY HORNY ARE WELCOME!

"Nope, don't see it."

I took a deep breath and put on my glasses.

As the acne-ridden teen with the sweating problem who lived through an exceptionally long ugly duckling phase, I developed a habit of removing my glasses as a way to avoid having a clear glimpse of my own face in the mirror. Finally, as I got older, I was able to take in my reflection without regretting what I saw.

I stared at myself. The acne was, for the most part, cleared up except for the few periodic signs of exam time stress. I had given up wearing makeup regularly and come to love my almond complexion, which had grown even more radiant in the Bermuda sun.

The irreverent naps on my head that once fought tirelessly against straightening and made me the butt of jokes were now harmoniously formed into a style that celebrated instead of attempting to tame them. My skinny minnie frame had finally balanced itself out with a woman's curves and a touch of sinewy definition that gave me an air of strength.

If it was no longer my looks that repelled the good, straight, non-criminal element, what was it? What was I doing wrong?

I looked at the Bermuda Botanical Gardens brochure that was sitting on my nightstand. A visit there would be a great way to take in more of the Island and make this a beautiful day.

The fact that I didn't feel so good didn't mean I couldn't look good. I changed into a black shirt and my black and white snake-print jeans. Then, I strapped on my inline skates with the idea of gliding part of the way down to the Botanical Gardens. First, though, I hit the boardwalk to see the beautiful rock and sea scenery.

Since this was technically winter, there were only a few other people on the beach jogging. The quiet, however, didn't make it feel any less vibrant. The sun had been shining relentlessly all morning with no clouds in sight. Minimal ocean breezes complimented the mild, sixty-five degree weather. Chattering birds passed overhead while swirls of sand went airborne on occasional gusts of wind. Bright red bromeliads added flashes of color to the dark gray, green, and blue aquascape ahead.

When I made it to the spot overlooking the cliff where Ali had found me a few days earlier, I began to understand why he thought I was probably a little off. In the full daylight, I could clearly see rock formations, several stories high, fixed at the shore.

The scene was no less captivating during the day, and I couldn't help but stay for a while. Once I was settled onto the sand, I slipped into a quiet, deep breathing exercise. Since my first night with Jack, I had discovered that even a few moments in meditation were enough to trigger that same ecstatic response. But with so many gloomy emotions swirling, the sensation didn't come easily.

I slowly swayed back and forth with the sounds of nature until I was abruptly interrupted.

"You back out here again?"

I opened my eyes and turned around. Ali was standing about ten feet away with his hands in his pockets and a confused look on his face. He just stared at me and chewed gum while I brushed myself off and stood up.

"You do realize that this is a resort. A vacation resort."

I waved my hand in the direction of the bay and went on.

"All of this, is the reason why all those little bungalows are filled to capacity, even in the middle of winter. Dare I say that it's the reason you have a job. Why is my presence here such a mystery to you?"

He looked out at the water, shrugged his shoulders as if he couldn't care less, then looked back at me and said, "Just seems strange."

I was convinced that he had another reason for sniffing me out every time I made a point of being alone, so I pressed him for an answer.

"What is it? I'm curious to know why you can't seem to stop following me around."

At this point I was standing almost toe-to-toe with him. Recognizing that he was dressed in plain clothes, I asked, "Are you even on duty right now?"

"I'm not, actually." he answered. "I live in one of the houses behind the resort, and this," he said pointing to the spot where I was sitting, "is where I usually relax after my morning run. I'm feeling a little territorial." He gave me a playfully suspicious look.

"Oh, well okay then. I was just getting ready to leave." I said smiling and rushing around to pick up my skates. I brushed the sand back and forth as if cleaning up after myself.

"The sand's already warm on that spot right there. It's pretty comfy. Don't mind me."

"Funny. Very funny. But I can adjust. It's not like I said you had to leave— unless you have somewhere to go."

"Actually, I'm sight-seeing today. So the beach is all yours."

"Where you going?"

"To the Botanical Gardens. I'm into flowers and… the outdoors and stuff."

"Oh." he said pointing his finger and looking off in the distance. "You'll like it. It's a favorite on the tour circuit."

I nodded.

"I know a guy who does aerial tours over the gardens. He's a helicopter pilot now but used to work security here when I first started. I could give you his number, but I might be able to get you a good deal if I call myself. Want me to call him?"

"Sure, thanks. A helicopter tour takes it up a notch."

"Cool." He dialed the number and waited for an answer.

"Tony! What's up, man? Hey, I got somebody interested in taking a flight today. She's going to be checking out the Botanical Gardens and I was thinking you could hook her up. Let me know as soon as you get this." He hung up and looked back at me.

"You know, " he said as if in deep thought, " he doesn't always get his messages right away when he's flying. And I wouldn't want you to miss out if you're going up that way today. I have to run some errands in that area a little later. I could meet you near the Botanical Gardens, just pop my head in his office or something. His assistant will get you going without a problem if I'm there."

"Umm… about what time would that be?" I asked.

"You know what?" he said with a snap of his finger, "I'm actually a tour guide during the high season."

I turned my lips up in disbelief.

"Is that right?"

"Yeah, and there's a really nice trail along the route you're taking. That is, if you don't mind foregoing the skating for a scenic hike."

"Mmm." I said.

"Not something I'd recommend you do by yourself, though, being a tourist." Ali put his hands back in his pockets and nodded his head slowly with a serene grin on his face.

I took one last look at the water. I was amused by his very subtle and nonchalant way of getting my attention. I silently bid the bay farewell for the time being.

"I guess I can't go wrong with a tour from an expert." I said.

He nodded again.

Then I asked, "And since somebody saw fit to hire you for security, I guess I can count on you not being a psycho?"

He gave me a look that implied that I already knew the answer to that question.

***

"So, I thought I heard you say something about classes a few days ago. Are you in school?" he asked.

"Yep."

"What's your major?"

"Architecture."

He raised his eyebrows. I never quite liked the way people always seemed surprised by that. I could understand why they would never have guessed someone like me would be studying architecture, but I never knew how to respond to their reaction.

I never felt like getting into an explanation of how more women and minorities were entering the field in record numbers. I hated sparking debates with prideful, middle-aged men about how "stupid" and "irresponsible" it was that someone with no money or connections and little academic grooming would go broke pursuing such a degree. I didn't even feel the need to smile confidently as if to say, *"Yeah, I know. Pretty amazing, right"* or something else that seemed arrogant. I just wanted to answer the question and move on.

"Wow!" Ali said. "How'd you become interested in that?"

"Well, I get a lot of cat calls around construction sites." I joked. "So I figured I'd get a kick out of walking around those places with instructions for the guys on how to do their jobs."

He laughed and went on, "Classes should be starting up pretty soon, right? My little cousin back in Louisiana just started a few days ago."

"Yeah, my classes start in another week."

"Cutting it close." he said.

I shrugged and said. "I work hard. I play hard." But something in me was saying,

"Yeah, right. When do you ever play?"

I searched for a way to change the subject.

"How about you? Is work your thing right now, or—"

"Yeah. I did school for a couple of years but never finished. I studied fine arts. Still do some sculpting on occasion. Wasn't totally sure which direction I wanted to go in so I came here to think and kind of stay out of trouble."

It was my turn to be surprised.

"Hmmm, what kind of trouble could a diligent advocate for order like yourself get into?"

I waited for an answer to my joke, but could see him shaking his head in avoidance of the question.

"So you're a fellow artist. What mediums do you prefer?"

"Mostly metals and clay." he said. "It's a real off and on thing, though. I just kinda go with it when it flows. I came here because one of my uncles retired here. He had a few extra rooms in his house and I wanted to be somewhere warm and nice with a less Spring Break-ish atmosphere. If I get bored, I get with some of my friends and do a weekend in Florida or on one of the other islands. But enough about me. I still can't figure out why you're here by yourself?"

"Why is that so odd?"

"You're on vacation. Most young ladies who come out here come during the high season for all of the festivals and stuff. Or, they come with their boyfriends."

"Mmm."

"So you got a boyfriend back home? I wouldn't think you'd be here alone if you did."

I remained quiet.

"That bad huh?" He shook his head. "Must have been a bad break up."

"You got it all figured out, huh?"

"I'm just guessing. It's the off season, classes start soon, you keep going around all incognito—"

"Incognito? Do I look like I'm hiding something?"

"I saw you slip out of the bungalow in your lil' dress last week. I just knew you were going to stop and get in a car with somebody, but you just kept walking off into the night."

"Everybody is so nosey around here! Okay, maybe I am a little on the weird side. I'll own that."

"I wouldn't say weird." Ali said, cutting me some slack. "... Eccentric."

I corrected him. "Eccentric is the smart person's word for weird."

"Oh, you think I'm smart too. Thank you! I'm flattered."

We both laughed.

"I'm just trying to piece it together," Ali said, "and I already know you like me so there's no harm in asking about your situation, right?"

"Whaaat? That's already been established?"

"It's cool." he said, "I'm just getting to the point."

I paused to gather my thoughts. His charm was intriguing, for sure.

"Well, I may like your packaging, but I don't know *you* from a can of paint."

"Yeah, right." he said, rolling his eyes and dismissing me.

"Here," he said pointing straight ahead, "this is the way to the Bermuda Railway Trail."

I was happy to be approaching a main attraction along the hike. We had already walked a couple of miles.

"Trains don't travel it anymore. They turned it into a walking trail because it has some of the best views of the islands."

We traveled for almost an hour along the trail then caught a bus to the botanical gardens. Once there, we roamed among thirty-six acres of trees, shrubs, and tropical flowers talking about the island, our backgrounds, and a bunch of other random topics that we stumbled on along the way. Several times, Ali had to stop me from groping flowers as I got carried away with their beauty and thoughtlessly tried to pick them.

Before I knew it, evening was approaching and we were strapping into our seats on his friend's helicopter and floating above the island.

"I wish Longwood Gardens in Pennsylvania did helicopter tours." I said. "That place is massive, like a thousand acres. That would be an awesome tour. I'd go on that tour like every season, just to see the changes. All those colorful patches of flowers probably look amazing from above."

"You're really into gardening. Have you studied landscape design?"

"Nah." I said. "This is strictly a hobby. Incorporating too much of the design process would make it feel, I dunno, inorganic. I could never make a job out of gardening. I love it too much."

"A lot of girls nowadays aren't into flowers. People think they're cheesy."

"Not me. I think they're sexy! You know Georgia O'Keefe's work?"

He just smiled and yelled, "Okay!" over the helicopter's propellers. "Then I guess you were all over that big delivery you just got."

"Huh?" I asked.

"That big delivery that came for you."

"What do you mean?"

He looked confused.

"You mean you didn't get it?"

"What was it?" I asked.

"There were some flowers at the front desk for you yesterday evening. You didn't get them?"

I shook my head and sat silently trying to figure out who would have sent me flowers while I was on vacation and why they would go so far out of their way. Only a few people back home knew that I was away, and I had given almost none of them the address. Then, I remembered sending Devi an email with the name of the resort, and I figured the flowers must be from her.

"Oh! They're probably from my friend, Devi." I said smiling and feeling like this trip was the best choice I'd made in years.

"Or that man you left in shambles," Ali said, "whoever he is."

I would have none of the thought, and I shook my head and laughed. Jack be gone!

Then I pulled a small ginger flower out of my pocket and said, "I guess I didn't need to steal this!"

His eyes popped as he laughed and said, "A flower klepto? Wow!"

***

As Ali and I approached my bungalow that evening I could see the flowers sitting next to my front door.

"Oh, look what finally showed up. It's huge!" I said inspecting the flowers in order to find a card. "Hmm, there's no card. I gotta call my friend ASAP and thank her."

"That's a pretty amazing bouquet for a vacation." Ali remarked.

"She's helping me through a few rough patches right now. She's, like, a life coach, but she's really more of a friend to me. That was really sweet of her."

"What are you doing tomorrow?" Ali asked.

"You tell me. I got nothing planned. I'm just hanging out."

"What have you already done?"

"Not much besides what you've seen me do."

"Oh, that's pitiful. Well, you got your cave tours. You could do horseback riding on the beach. There's watersports. I'm not a big yoga and meditation person, but that seems like it might be down your alley. I don't have to work until tomorrow evening. I could take you to check out Beluga in Hamilton for lunch, if you want. It's a popular sushi restaurant."

"What time you want to meet up?" I asked.

"I'll stop by around eleven thirty."

"Alright. See you later." I turned to unlock my door when Ali added one more thing.

"Oh, Jane... you really should keep your blinds closed if you're gonna walk around, ya know, free as a bird."

I winced and did a couple of neck rolls to relieve some sudden tension before turning toward him again.

"How much did you see, exactly?"

"Me? Oh no, I didn't see you. Mr. Clayton next door did. He told me about it this morning when I went for my run. He wasn't complaining or anything, but you should probably be more careful next time."

Relieved, I answered, "Well, thank you very much for that advice."

He had one good laugh at my expense then left. I dragged the floral arrangement into the bungalow. It was an elegant, hourglass-shaped, ceramic vase with a matte black finish. It was about twenty inches high and stuffed to the gills with tropical flowers and palm leaves. I sat down to give Devi a call.

"Are you getting lost in paradise?" she asked upon answering.

"Almost! It is so relaxing here and I feel so rejuvenated and alive. This place is beautiful. And I had to call you right away to thank you for the flowers. This arrangement is gorgeous!"

"What flowers?"

"You didn't send me flowers?"

"No. Girl, what man you done got tied up with already?"

"Uh."

I looked around while my brain scanned for possible answers and avoided the obvious.

Then I said, "You know what? It could've been my girls from back home. They know this last year was pretty tough for me and they probably got together to get me a surprise. Actually, Devi, I just got in and I want to get a little writing done then bed down early tonight. Is there a good time I can call you this weekend?"

"You can call me tomorrow or Sunday. You know later is better. I'm a night owl."

"Okay, I'm looking forward to it. Got plenty to talk about! Take care."

"You too, hon."

I knew full well that my peeps back home, loving as they were, would not have shelled out the money for flowers that easily cost over two-hundred dollars to purchase and ship.

I was feeling too lighthearted to stress over it, so I didn't allow myself to consider what the other possibility could be.

"Never mind all that."

I made up my mind that I wanted to tackle cave exploration next with Ali, so I showered and got into bed for a wonderful night's sleep. Then the bedside phone rang.

"It must be Ali giving me a few more details for tomorrow", I thought.

"Hello?" I answered.

Silence.

"Hello-o?"

I peeped the caller ID and realized that the number was unidentified. Then I heard static buzzing over a muffled voice. I figured it was a wrong number or bad connection and hung up.

I stretched out on the bed and stared straight through the curtains at the moon, then wished it goodnight.

15

Peeking through the side of the shades in my bedroom window, I could see Mr. Clayton having his morning cup of coffee. He was sitting at a little bistro table in the bay window that faced the rose bushes between our kitchens. His plaid robe hung open and its belt drooped onto the floor, barely clinging to one of the robe's belt loops. He squinted at his paper through glasses that must have been nearly half an inch thick. I yanked open the shades and jumped back to avoid being seen.

These new surroundings were making me a bit more playful and daring than usual. I was planning something that I would never have tried back home around people who I'd have to see every day. Nope, the receptionist would definitely not let this kind of prank past her desk back in Philly. But, she was on vacation, and I could feel myself growing freer by the day. I wanted to seize this chance to take some power back from Mr. Clayton.

I ran to the kitchen window. Sure enough, there he was, standing at his window, gripping his robe shut and bobbing his head up and down, straining to see into my bedroom. He stayed there for exactly one hundred and sixteen seconds— I counted— waiting for me to surface. So I did.

I yanked open the kitchen blinds and opened a bottle of water to get my gears grinding for the day. Standing in the buff, with my back to the window, I chugged the whole bottle while giving Mr. Clayton a fully unobstructed view of my toned shoulders, gracefully curved lower back and round glutes. Then I threw the bottle in the trashcan and walked slowly back down the hall.

"Now go tell that." I said aloud as I stepped into the shower.

***

The doorbell rang not a minute too late— right at eleven thirty. I answered wearing fitted dark jeans, a white crochet top that draped off one shoulder with a white tank top underneath, and crisp white Pumas.

The moment the door opened I heard the panting of an approaching canine, and in ran a young golden retriever with a disheveled yellow rose in his mouth. Before Ali could grab him he ran two circles around my living room and back toward the door as if he would finally obey.

He peed over the threshold.

I smacked the puppy on the back and told him to stay outside. Ali stood there nervously searching for something to say.

"You got any paper towels?" he asked.

Just then, Mr. Clayton walked by and looked between the trees to see what was going on.

"Oh, what's up, man? Uh, that's your dog?"

Ali said, "No, I'm watching him for my neighbor."

Ali looked back at me to see just how angry I might be getting. I am not a dog person.

Mr. Clayton went on trying to strike up a conversation.

"Yeah, I saw him run up on the bushes. I didn't know if he was a stray or what. Looks young. Better get a collar on him quick. He'll train well if you get him some Beggin' Strips. That's what I use with my dogs."

"I'll be sure to let his owner know about that. His leash just snapped off and he went flying. I don't even know where it went."

"Heh, heh!" Mr. Clayton laughed and stood there awkwardly peering through the bushes before finally deciding to leave.

I headed into the kitchen for cleaning supplies but caught a glimpse of Mr. Clayton giving Ali an enthusiastic double thumbs up before he walked off. Ali smiled bashfully back at him then snapped back to cleaning after I noticed it.

"Maybe he shouldn't come with us to the cave after all." Ali said. He opened the trashcan to throw away the paper towels.

"Are you serious?" I yelled. "If you don't take your trifling self outside and find somewhere else to trash that mess… No, he needs to stay outside." I shouted as he tried to quietly bring the dog inside. "Outside!"

"But I wanted you to meet him." Ali said. "He followed me home a few weeks ago, but I wasn't into having a pet. My neighbor took him but I named him Pops."

I couldn't help but to be curious.

"Why Pops?"

"Like the cereal? Corn Pops!"

Ali said that as if it was something I should already know. His face practically lit up when he said it. I immediately thought that any grown man who could get that excited over cereal was bound to present some unique challenges.

"Doesn't his color look just like the color of Corn Pops?" Ali asked.

"Probably more like Corn Flakes." I said, giving the dog another look.

Giving in, I gestured for him to come inside and he walked over and sat next to me.

"You should have all that pee out of your system by now, right, Pops?"

I turned to Ali shaking my head and said,

"See, I don't like the way that sounds. You sound like Lamont from *Sanford and Son*. 'Pop! Pop!'"

"It's not Pop, though. It's Pops."

"Still doesn't sound right. Makes him sound old and decrepit."

Normally, I would have never given someone such a hard time over something that was completely their prerogative, but I liked picking on Ali.

"Well I'm not calling him Flakes." Ali said.

"That's your business. So what's up with lunch, because I don't know if this restaurant is friendly to untrained dogs."

"I'll take him back home before we go eat. I wanted you to meet him. I thought about taking him to the cave with us, but considering his leash handling, that might not be a good idea. He seems to like you, though."

I smiled and gave Pops barely a pat on the head as we headed out the door for our adventure.

"That's my first line of defense." Ali said with that suspicious-but-not-really glance. "If his senses say you're okay, you're probably okay."

I stared back at him and simply said, "Shut up!"

***

"So, how does a college student end up with a life coach?" Ali asked after we placed our orders at Beluga.

This question surprised me. I was used to heavy doses of small talk with new men, but I guess we'd already covered so much ground the day before. We had already talked about his life in Bermuda, attractions around the islands, projects we'd worked on, and pieces he'd created whenever he was in an artistic mood.

I guess Katrina was right, in a way. I did always feel awkward talking to new guys. I feared not having a clue of what a guy might want to talk about. I just prepared more questions to build on our previous conversation, about his future plans and even his experiences with tourists. But Ali only seemed interested in knowing more about me.

"She's a lot of things." I answered. "But first, I guess, she's a good friend of mine. She hosts one of my favorite internet radio shows about women and relationships and stuff. I called into the show once, and I've been talking with her ever since. She's like, twice my age, so her perspective on a lot of things is crystal clear."

"You listen to talk radio?"

"Yeah, what's wrong with that?"

Ali grinned and said, "Nothing. How old *are* you?"

I chuckled and said, "Twenty-four. What about you?"

"I couldn't really peg your age. You look kind of young, but you act older. I'm twenty-one."

Hearing him say he was twenty-one was a little jarring. They say girls mature faster than guys. Even the ones my age acted like babies. What was I supposed to do with a younger one?

"I get that a lot." I said. "Don't really know what to make of it."

"I didn't mean anything bad by it. It was a compliment. Seems like you've got things in order. You're in school. Got your own place. You're chilling on a nice vacation before going back to classes. You don't seem to have that shallow, party girl vibe. You probably keep a spotless place and a balanced checkbook too. "

"Ha! Except I have a life coach!"

"Yeah, what's your deal? Your bungalow is pristine. Who keeps things this clean on vacation? And I saw that Bible on the counter in your bungalow. You into church?"

"Yeah, but it's more than a church thing. It's really what keeps me together."

"I can see that. You can get pretty worked up, but there also seems to be something different about you. Something kind of quiet and peaceful."

"It's made me a lot more self-aware. How about you? Any spiritual leanings?"

"When I was young," he said, "my mom was Seventh Day Adventist, but we were never totally into it. We stopped going to services when I was like six. I've read stuff about different religions, but nothing seems to really stand out for me."

"My dad was totally nonreligious." I said. "But my mom was a very devout Christian for most of my life. She kept us in church. When I was fourteen, I just felt compelled to do something about all that stuff I had been taught. I was old enough to know right from wrong and thought I couldn't avoid being held accountable for any mistakes I might make. I saw what my surroundings had to offer, and I didn't want to get caught up. I don't know. It just hit me, like, yo, I have a destiny and I don't want to waste any time on this foolishness. I was thinking about all the things I wanted for myself and knew God had to come first. It was just time to wake up and get serious."

I didn't want to make it sound like I was trying to shove religion down his throat, but I felt an obligation to represent for my faith.

"So, like, what was that like having a mom who was religious and a dad who wasn't?"

"You know, you ask a lot of questions."

I didn't want to show it, but his genuine interest was comforting. He smiled and waited for my answer.

"Well," I said, "it was interesting, to say the least."

I tried reading Ali's body language. He was calm, looking straight at me, and not showing signs of being distracted or weirded out by my talking. He seemed truly interested in knowing more about my background, and asked questions quicker than I could turn the tables and ask him any.

I remembered the condition he caught me in a few nights ago. Maybe he was trying to diffuse what he thought was a situation teetering on a breaking point. I didn't mind that, and would take this opportunity to open up in a way that I had wanted to for a long time.

"My dad has problems with addiction."

"Oh." he said with a look of surprise. "Has he gotten any treatment or anything?"

"He's done a few rounds of rehab, and I think he gains perspective with each try. We just pray for him and try to support him however we can. "

"How long has it been a problem for him?"

"He's been drinking for years, but got into drugs when he was in the army, back in the eighties."

"Oh," Ali nodded. "right when that crack thing was getting out of control."

"Yeah. Right before that, when they were seniors in high school, my mom got pregnant with my brother and he wasn't really ready to be tied down. But because his parents were old school, you know, it was a shotgun marriage kind of deal. He claimed she got pregnant on purpose and always blamed her for it. So let's just say there was a lot more going on than just the religious differences between my mom and dad."

I stopped talking, but realized that Ali hadn't taken his eyes off me. It was as if the mention of my dad's problems had completely captured him. He'd stopped chewing for a moment when I mentioned the drugs. I wondered if he had a relative or friend with similar issues. He waited for me to say something else.

"My dad— his name is Miles— has always been a really strong-willed kind of guy. He never wore a wedding ring. Never got my mom one. Rarely ever went out with us, not even to the grocery store. For our entire childhood. My mom even told me that he once said he didn't believe in the concept of marriage, whatever that means. Have you ever heard guys say that? I figured that was a guy thing."

"No. How long were they married?" Ali asked.

"Twenty-four years total. Can you believe that? He would come home from work every day and make everybody leave the living room so he could watch TV alone. He was usually pretty irritable."

Ali's grave facial expression remained unchanged as I rambled on, not realizing just how much my guard was disintegrating. Eventually, it didn't occur to me that I needed to hold anything back.

"Seemed like my parents used to argue all the time. As he got deeper into the drugs, he became violent more often. My brother, Terrence, would jump in to protect my mom.

"He would talk a bunch of crap to my brother trying to intimidate him to see what he would do. His idea was to toughen him up before the streets or the *"white man"* got him, so he said. But the truth was, he'd never gotten to know him well enough to realize that wasn't necessary."

Ali's interest didn't wane so I continued. It felt like a faucet, or some emotional fire hydrant had been released in me, and I couldn't stop.

"He'd go through these spells where we could feel his mood was heating up and we knew a fight was coming. It was in the air— the way the air thickens before a big storm. He would talk and talk about his childhood, and eventually he'd get so mad that he just had to fight somebody. Sometimes the police would come, but my mom would never tell the cops what actually happened once they showed up. Didn't want to *'turn a black man over to the white man'*, I guess. A lot of black women think like that.

"One time when I was little and they were separated, he found out that my mom was seeing this dude. Now, despite the fact that he had done plenty of running around on her, he was jealous. Went down to the guy's job at the shipyard chasing him around with a crow bar and a butcher knife. I don't know how he avoided getting arrested that day.

"Well my mom heard about what he did earlier that day, so she put us in the bed with her at night. She thought he wouldn't hurt her too bad in front of us. All I remember is lying in their bed under this turquoise light. Instead of a regular white light bulb, they kept a turquoise light bulb in the overheard fixture in their room. It was that 70's décor, like those beaded curtains everybody used to have."

"Anyway, I could hear him coming up the steps, not saying a word. Then I saw the shadow of that knife on the blue-tinted wall. That blade was like eight or nine inches long. He walked into her closet and started ripping her clothes up."

Ali sat up and placed my hand in his.

"Did you or your brother say anything?" He asked. "I mean, how old were you? You must have been so scared."

I pulled my hand away.

"I was five. My brother, Terrence, was nine. He was asleep. Honestly, I might have been scared then, but now I only remember the adrenaline. I guess deep down I thought he wouldn't hurt any of us, but that he just needed to show his anger. Anyway, by then, I was kind of used to the drama. Every time something happened, it was like a show."

"Drugs can really make monsters out of people." Ali said, shaking his head.

"Yeah but Miles had issues long before the drugs."

Ali, still on the edge of his seat, nearly dropped his food off his fork because he was watching me so carefully as I talked. My self-protection instinct finally kicked then. I didn't want to be the only one spilling my guts, so I tried to quickly wrap up my spiel.

"Anyway, they're divorced now."

"What made your mom finally leave? Was it an incident or, like, an accumulation of stuff?"

"Actually, he was the one who left. Once I graduated high school, he figured his job was done."

"Man." I could tell he was searching for words so I distracted myself by trying to find another shrimp on my plate. The food at Beluga was delicious but I'd lost my sense of taste after telling my story.

"But, there had to be some good times." Ali said. "I mean, my dad wasn't around when I was growing up, so I always figured it would have been better to have a crazy dad than to not have one at all. What about all the times when he wasn't, you know, like that?"

"That's why mom called him Dr. Jekyll/ Mr. Hyde. And that's what made his addiction struggle so hard to watch. He wasn't a family man— we'd accepted that very early on. But he had this other side that was downright brilliant. He's an extremely talented painter and graphic artist. He could sit here and draw your portrait in 10 minutes and it would look just like you.

"He's really smart, too. One of the best debaters I've ever seen. That actually could've been a good thing if he knew how to do it peacefully.

"He always takes this objective stance on things. Like, he maintains this air of not being beholden to anything, so he can see everything with almost no bias. He gets his facts straight. I've seen him wear preachers down on subject after subject— everything from the need for tithing to going to church on Sundays. Some would leave the conversation with their heads hung in shame."

Ali smiled.

"And he was always cracking jokes. Had us rolling even when we thought we shouldn't be. The jokes seemed kind of mean, but his timing was impeccable. There was this local news anchor with a little speech problem and bug eyes. Miles had met him in a grocery store once, tried to say hello, and the guy just kept walking without even acknowledging his hand. I'll never forget… his name was Antwon James. Whenever the news came on, Miles would say, *'Oh, there's Antwerp! Looking like a bull frog.'* Then he'd start singing *Jeremiah was a Bullfrog* and bug his eyes all out. You had to be there!"

Ali stopped me.

"What do you call him?"

"Who?" I asked.

"Your dad, his name's Miles, right?"

"Right."

"Why do *you* call him Miles?"

"Because that's his name."

"You always call him that?"

"Since I was a kid. It's like that on his side of the family. He calls his parents by their names, we call him by his name. It's just how we do."

"Come on, you were his little girl, right? That didn't soften his edges at all?"

I laughed and said, "Not Miles Luck! Son, daughter—didn't matter. He wouldn't let anybody change him."

I felt my heart start to beat a little faster and sweat forming in my armpits. I stuffed a hunk of Mahi Mahi in my mouth and started chugging juice, hoping Ali wouldn't notice my sudden nervousness.

In telling Ali about my family drama, I felt detached, even a little amused, as if telling someone else's sordid tale of dysfunction. It was a big, therapeutic release, really. It was different from talking to Devi, because Ali was someone who didn't have to listen. He hadn't established himself as a guardian-like figure for me or someone who was being paid for their services.

The part about being my father's daughter made me uncomfortable. Just as uncomfortable as I had always felt in Miles' presence. I didn't want that to show. I regretted telling Ali anything at all.

***

The story of being Miles' daughter was full of tangled feelings, confusion, and contradictions. My life with him had simultaneously made me an empathetic human being who longed to see others at peace and a cold woman who could shut her heart down in an instant when necessary. Several images of us in that living room flashed like Polaroids in my mind as Ali waited for me to tell him more.

From my dad, I learned how to get a little attention out of him without getting too close. I'd sit on the loveseat rather than right next to him on the couch. If I had to sit on the same couch with him, I was sure our arms did not touch.

I also become an agent of damage control, the one who tried to clean up the bad vibes and lighten the mood at home in between incidents. Because I already had a bubbly personality, I usually decided to be funny.

If he was sitting depressed in front of the TV after blowing through another paycheck, I'd put on a goofy grin and do some silly dance in the middle of the living room hoping to make him laugh. If we talked, I tried to keep a pleasant, non-threatening look on my face. I kept the conversation superficial so he wouldn't feel like I was prying. I learned to keep my desire for his attention in check and in doing so, was ironically able to squeeze out some approval here and there.

But as I got older, my need to know him and to have him fully know and understand me only grew. In taking responsibility for my own life, I thought trying to make things better at home was also my Christian duty.

Sitting there in front of Ali, this man I'd just met, telling my story, I was transported to the passenger side of my mom and dad's old car (the green Plymouth Volare that was gone a year later, lost to drug debt like one or two of our other cars). I was fourteen and Miles was driving me home from a high school bible club meeting.

I was preparing to confront him about the state of our family.

Halfway through the ride across the highway, I waited, stared at the pavement outside, then at the trees. I had to get him before he cemented himself back down in front of that TV and while I had the words properly rehearsed. I gulped, ignored the pounding in my chest, and began:

"Miles, can you turn the radio down for a minute?"

"Say what? Hol' up. Lemme turn this down. What you say?"

I went in.

"You know, I've been thinking about how we don't spend much time together as a family. In church, we talk about the importance of family and stuff, and I thought it would be nice if we did more together. You could come to the movies sometimes with us, or to the beach or the park.

"You and Ma could do those kinds of things together, like on her birthday. Instead of ordering takeout on weekends, we could go out to Golden Corral, or something."

He kept his right hand at the six o'clock position on the wheel and looked ahead as I spoke. I looked at his hands out of the corner of my eye to get a gauge for his mood, then gazed at the road ahead.

"It'd be nice to have you involved more. You know, maybe you could come to some of Terrence's tennis matches or practice with him sometimes. I know he's not really into the same kind of stuff as you, but it's important for a dad to have some one-on-one time with his son… and his daughter."

I didn't know exactly how he'd respond. I hadn't daydreamed about that part. I had prayed on it the night before and simply hoped for the best.

In order to prevent him from completely shutting me out, I avoided hitting him with anything too heavy.

"I'm starting to get scared because I feel like I'll never know you. I feel like I'm missing out on something important, and I don't know how to deal with these men who are starting to pay attention to me."

That was the part I kept to myself. I also didn't tell him how rejected I felt as a little girl whose dad pushed her away when she tried to sit in his lap, or how weird it always felt to have a dad right there in the next room but feeling like he was worlds away. I didn't tell him that I'd written a letter to my youth pastor expressing gratitude for his hugging me and asking how I was doing after every Wednesday night bible study. I didn't tell him that my youth pastor felt like a dad to me, and that being in his presence was a relief because he never made me feel nervous or afraid.

I held out the hope of being heard. If I made an appeal that was non-threatening and didn't sound too much like an accusation, maybe he'd bend.

But he didn't. He stopped for a red light and turned the radio all the way down.

"Lemme tell you something, cuz I know yo' mama put you up to this. You need to stop listenin' to everything them people at the church say. We ain't the Brady Bunch!" He let up on the brakes and then eased across an intersection four blocks from our apartment.

"We doin' alright. Yeah, I drink and I do what I do, but it could be a lot worse, okay! Y'all know what went on in my house when I was growing up, right? RIGHT?!"

Tears welled in my eyes but I fought their descent. I stared out the passenger side window, creating an invisible shield between me and the ranting man next to me. I prayed a tear wouldn't drop onto my cheek. If he saw it, he would only rant longer.

"Yep." I answered.

"OK, then. So as long as y'all got a roof over y'all head, some food on the table and nobody molestin' or knocking you upside the head, you doin' alright. Me and your mama don't be fightin', we be talkin'. That's what grown folks do. Everything ain't always hunky dory. My dad wasn't all lovey dovey with his kids. So y'all need to stop tryin' to make me something I'm not. Fathers and daughters don't need to be close, and I don't need to be close to you."

In that moment, for the first time, I found my heart's shutoff valve. I understood that there was nothing I could do about him and that it wasn't my fault. I couldn't waste any more time trying. He turned the music back up. I stopped crying and never bothered him again.

***

Ali ordered dessert while I chewed up and slowly swallowed the last bite of my sushi. I was enjoying his company but feared I'd chased him away with my story. The discomfort, the uncertainty and suspicion I felt around most men— that same nervousness that I always felt with Miles— was absent with Ali. It was a marvelously strange feeling, one that I could get used to.

16

"Hold up!" Ali called out. "We're here."

When we got to the entrance to Admiral's Cave I almost walked past it.

"Huh?" I said in disbelief.

"This is it. The entrance to the cave is a sinkhole."

I looked down at my clothes and said, "Come again? Ali, you didn't bother to tell me that I needed to dress for crawling into the center of the earth."

"You didn't know you needed to dress down more?"

"Ali, I thought you were taking me to one of the more public, more touristy caves with prepared pathways and... lights." I eyed the sinkhole, which looked like it led to a dangerous abyss.

As upbeat as ever, he grabbed his book bag and pulled out two helmets outfitted with LEDs. I put one on, then he handed me a light jacket and some waterproof pants to put on over my jeans. After I put these on, he handed me a pair of gloves.

"It's cool, don't worry about it. Just watch your step and follow my instructions. There's no guided tours here, so it should be pretty quiet."

We slowly made our own way down the sinkhole into the cavern as he explained some of its features.

"Admiral's cave is a dry cave, it's above the water table. Wet caves are below the water table, at least partially, and can be more complex and difficult to access. You know it can take one hundred years for one cubic inch of a stalactite to form?"

"Amazing!" I said, shining my light on rock formations that were thousands of years old.

We moved forward slowly, stopping often to admire the beauty of the surreal space.

"I assumed ground heat would keep a place like this warm, but it is pretty cool down here." I said. "I'm glad you brought me some extra clothes."

I smiled and turned to find Ali smiling back at me. We walked on and eventually reached a point where the path was slippery and inconsistent. He took my hand and quietly walked beside me for a minute before suggesting we take a break.

We found a spot to sit down. Ali turned on a large flood light and shined it on the wall opposite us. The rocky surface still looked as though it was oozing, with reddish brown turning to purple and then to black as light bounced off its bumps and disappeared into its recesses.

"It's surprisingly comfortable." I said. "I thought being in a place like this might feel claustrophobic, but it's so expansive."

"Yeah, it is really nice. I wish we had time to check out one of the more popular caves before you leave, though. Proper lighting and planned paths really help you to see the best of these caves. This place has been vandalized a little and it's more for people who like to go off the touristy path."

"That's perfect, as far as I'm concerned. Coming down here and discovering it ourselves makes it that much better, right? Trail mix?"

"What's in it?" He asked.

"Peanuts, almonds, cashews, Craisins, chocolates. I made it myself."

"Cool. Here, I have some water."

He scooted up next to me and we kept talking.

"So when you moved up to Philly, was that something you did to get away from home?"

"Not really." I admitted. "It was never my plan to be that far from home. I had my eye on Virginia Tech. I busted my butt in high school, stayed out of trouble, got good grades and had a one track-mind to become an architect. That was it. There was no other option. I had been fascinated with that profession since I was, like, eight, and I wanted it more than almost anything."

"I wanted to be teacher." Ali said after thinking for a moment. "Then a fire fighter. Where'd you get architect from, see it in the movies?"

We both laughed knowing that my exposure to the profession as a kid was pretty limited.

"No, it was construction around my neighborhood. I used to round up a couple of my friends and try to break into these new houses that were being built. The smell of the wood, the sound of buzzing saws— the whole scene was amazing. I got hooked on *Bob Vila Home Again,* which used to come on Saturday mornings. After Saturday morning cartoons, I was gonna learn to remodel bathrooms! I always wanted to build. Then somewhere along the way I figured it would be better to design. I wasn't trying to be out on anybody's roof!

"I took the PSAT's in tenth grade. The results got sent to this college in Philly, Farmont U, and they invited me for a visit that summer. My parents put up some of the money and I raised the rest with the help of my high school mentor, Ms. Macey. She was the sponsor for the bible club I was president of.

"We gave letters to the faculty and I sold candy in the teacher's lounge to raise the money. That summer I was in Philly, touring a major city for the first time, learning about architecture and lovin' it!"

"So that's how you ended up in Philly?" Ali remarked.

"Not quite." I said. "Even after that, it was still all about Virginia Tech. And I got in. I got some scholarships and other financial aid, but it didn't cover everything. One month before Freshman Transition, my parents sat me down on the living room couch and told me that they were not letting me go."

"Not *letting* you go?" Ali asked, baffled.

"I guess, until then, they'd hoped that I'd lose the fantasy and not actually do what I'd been planning all those years. They straight up sat there and told me that one, the school and the field I was pursuing were predominantly white, and they didn't think I could withstand the challenge; two, that if that white school really wanted me there they would have given me a full scholarship; and three, that because I was so young and naïve, they were afraid I'd get hooked up with some athlete and come home pregnant."

Ali leaned back as if someone had let the air out of him. "Are you serious? Why didn't they have that talk with you when you first started applying to colleges?"

"They really weren't a part of that process. They were encouraging, but they had never gone through it themselves. I had mentors to help with that stuff. And it's crazy, because I didn't have a rebellious bone in my body back then. I never even considered ways to go against their wishes, to find the money on my own. I didn't even realize I could have. And then I wondered, what if they were right?"

"Yeah," Ali said, "because Christians are really big on 'honor your father and mother' and 'obey your parents' and all that, right?"

"Exactly. I didn't have long to think about it, either. I wasn't gonna start school late, so I enrolled in ODU's civil engineering program. That school was only thirty minutes from where we lived. I remembered my high school vice principal telling me to study engineering instead of architecture, because *'the job market would be more favorable for a black female.'* I guess he called himself trying to warn me.

"Anyway, I spent a few semesters there being bored to death with computer programming classes, failing chemistry, and getting more and more miserable. I wasn't cut out to be an engineer. So I finally decided to apply to Fairmont. ODU didn't offer an architecture program, and my grades were so bad at that point, I couldn't transfer to another local school with the program. I didn't care how many loans I had to take out, I was just gonna get there! And I had fallen in love with Philly anyway, so I figured I couldn't go wrong."

For the first time, the expression that Ali directed toward me was one of admiration.

"Thank God, off the pity pot!"

"It was crazy because so many people's parents pressure them to go to college, be a doctor, be a lawyer, do something big. My parents pressured us to be average. I guess they didn't want us to be disappointed."

Ali kept chewing and shook his head. "Well what about your mom now? How's she been since the divorce?"

I looked up at the wall wondering if he could handle any more. "She remarried." I said dropping my head a little.

"How's that working out." he asked.

"Her husband's in prison."

"What?!"

"You know what," I said sitting up straight, "let's not even go there now. I think I've told you enough of my friggin' life story. I honestly can't believe you wanted to sit through all that."

"Not a problem for me." he said. "I don't have to live it. Kudos to you for making it this far."

"But for the grace of God." I said.

Just then, I heard the faint sound of footsteps.

"How often do people come down here?" I asked him as he looked in the same direction.

"I dunno. It's not a show cave, so visitation is pretty random. If somebody else does show up, they're probably just exploring like us. Nothing to worry about."

We ate more trail mix. Then I heard what sounded like dense crystal crashing against the cave floor.

"Okaaay." I said, looking in the direction of the noise and trying to appear unafraid.

Ali looked calmly at me then shined the flood light down the path.

"Was probably just a falling rock in one of the chambers."

"Falling rock? That doesn't sound very reassuring."

"We're fine." Ali insisted.

We got comfortable again, just before hearing another crack then a crash. This time it sounded closer.

Ali was noticeably annoyed and yelled down the cavern.

"There's an officer with Bermuda Police down here. Keep it up! It will be some serious trouble if I get my hands on your ass!"

He turned back toward me.

"Probably some dumb kids breaking off the rocks for keepsakes."

Just when we thought the vandals had gotten the point, we heard the sound again— three more broken stalactites. Ali sighed then motioned for me to stand up with him.

He moved forward slowly, shining the flood light ahead. I stayed close behind him. Then, as we reached the midpoint between our perch and the cave entrance, we heard what sounded like footsteps, but they didn't seem to be coming from the direction of the entrance.

"Did you hear that?" I asked in a whisper.

"Yeah. Sometimes the sound gets thrown a little bit."

Ali looked behind us and listened carefully, then the footsteps picked up speed.

He called out, "Ay, anybody else down here?"

There was another, even louder crack.

"What's up?! Easy with the rocks, man! There's other people down here!"

The next crack was accompanied by the remnant of a rock which was thrown across the cave floor and landed a few feet from us.

"What the—!" Ali looked quickly at me, then back at the rock.

"Go, go, go! Let's just go." I whispered, fear dripping from each word.

"No! We can't run in here! You crazy? Just chill."

As another rock came our way, Ali bent down to pick up one nearby.

"Just watch your step and keep moving forward. We'll be back at the entrance soon."

We moved quickly toward the entrance, both stopping several times to hurl rocks into the blackness. Right before navigating the sinkhole opening, one of Ali's rocks made contact with the mystery person, and we could hear him let out a deep mannish groan.

We walked quickly toward the main road and caught a cab back to the resort.

"You think he'll report us to the cops for hitting him?" I asked.

"He was following *us*. Plus, I don't think he even saw us all that well."

"Yeah, but how bad do you think he was hurt?"

"Jane, those fools who do stuff like that, they don't run to the cops when something happens. They're troublemakers. They're the last people to call the cops for something. Anyway, I'm sorry for taking you down there. I've never known there to be any problems like that."

"It's not your fault. It's a beautiful site. I'm glad we went. Plus, we gave a lot better than we got!"

"First stealing, now assault." he said smiling. "I'ma have to turn in my badge because of you."

"Rent-a-cop!" I joked back. "What badge?"

17

As we arrived back at the resort I glanced at my watch and opened the door to my bungalow.

"Oh, it's only six o'clock." I said. "It's dinner time. You hungry?"

I sucked my teeth when I saw Mr. Clayton walk by again waving at me and Ali.

"I'll be inside." I said.

Mr. Clayton had slowed down as he approached us. Ali greeted him politely.

"How you doing, Mr. Clayton?"

"Good, good! Uh, hello, young lady."

I threw up one hand as I walked into the bungalow. I'm certain he didn't realize that I could still hear him as I made my way to the kitchen to prepare dinner.

"Beautiful evening." he said, staring at Ali with his hands folded. "You… uh… you staying here tonight?"

"Here? Oh, nah. We just went to see one of the caves. I was supposed to work tonight but somebody else took over my shift for me. We just chillin', you know."

"Oh, is Darnell working?"

"No. Kenny. It'll be Kenny making the rounds tonight. Okay, Mr. Clayton, you enjoy your evening out there."

"Alright, Ali! You enjoy your night off." Mr. Clayton attempted to lower his voice. "And if you do decide to stay here tonight… umm… leave them shades open."

He backed away slowly with his eyebrows raised, as if he assumed there was some unspoken understanding between them. Ali glared back at him.

"What did that fool say?" I asked as Ali walked inside. "Friggin' perv!"

"Never mind that. What's this you said about dinner? You wanna go to the resort restaurant?"

"No, actually I'm going to do a little something."

He took a step backward and looked around the kitchen.

"You're going to do what? You cooking? Do I need to call the fire department?"

"No you do not!"

"I mean, I got a couple of friends down there. They can come by just in case."

"You assuming I can't cook because I'm a college chick?"

"No, I'm actually looking at your slim frame and wondering how much you eat, much less how well you cook."

"I'm a very healthy weight, thank you. And the fact that I'm in good shape should be a sign to you that my diet and my cooking are great. Just shut up and turn on the TV. I already had some stuff defrosted in the fridge, so this won't take long."

"Who cooks their own food on vacation?"

"Somebody who enjoys it and does it well."

I breezed around the kitchen preparing grilled rockfish with an herb and butter sauce, spicy couscous, and cucumber and tomato salad. I gave him a plate then sat down across from him to enjoy mine.

"That was quick!"

"Mmm hmm. That's because I know what I'm doing."

He flipped through a few channels while I poured us both a glass of white wine. He stopped for a few seconds on a channel where a commercial for a local circus was playing.

"I'm not a fan of circuses." he said abruptly. "I hate to see the animals acting all cooperative like that. You know that shit ain't natural."

He caught me looking at him and quickly apologized for his language.

"Oh, I'm sorry. I mean, it's not natural."

"I was just waiting for you to elaborate."

The phone rang before he could finish.

I picked it up without a second thought and said, "Hello."

Whoever was on the other end did not say anything.

"Hello-o!"

Finally, Jack responded.

"Enjoyin' your trip?"

I hung up and sat back down to crack jokes with Ali about the horrible acting in the cheesy, low budget drama we were watching. Then the phone rang again.

As soon as I picked up,

"You hanging up on me now?!"

"I saw your missed calls on my cell phone. I'm not ready to talk right now."

I was having such a good, peaceful time in Bermuda. I wanted no reminders of what awaited back home, so much so that I didn't even say his name when I spoke to him.

Ali put his glass down and slowly turned to face me.

"I think I been waitin' long enough for you, Jane."

"...This isn't my cell. How did you get this number?"

"Look, I just want to talk to you."

"I'm sorry but I can't right now."

I hung up again and then stood with my hands on my hips staring at the phone.

"Problem?" Ali asked.

I crossed my arms and shook my head in frustration.

"It's nothing. You want more food?"

"He's from back home? I knew it." Ali said with a hint of sympathy. "What you do to that man, Jane?"

"Oh you don't even know who the heck he is, but you're just going to assume I did something to him?"

Ali smiled. "Are you one of those chicks?" he then asked in a suspicious tone. "Is this what you do? Just travel around making a mess of every man you meet. I hope I'm not next."

"Next at what?! Who do you think *you* are?" I asked, getting a little heated. "You know what, forget it."

"I'm just joking."

"Yeah, because you clearly think this is some kind of joke."

"Alright." Ali gave in. "You tell me your side of the story."

I plopped back on the couch and stared at Ali a while before deciding not to tell him anything about Jack.

Somehow, instead, the conversation segued into another long, drawn out story. It was about the last time I'd found myself in the clutches of a guy who didn't want to let go.

"It happened when I studied abroad. He was this quiet, short, scrawny, brooding type who you could tell was a little unhinged by the look in his eyes. We were placed in the same research group together, and after a few days of work, he got all attached to me. Kept saying God told him I was supposed to be his wife. So whenever we all went to dinner as a group or on an outing, he'd sit across from me or next to me or right behind me on the bus."

Ali shook his head, still side-eying me like he questioned my honesty.

"One day, after class, he ran up behind me and planted himself in front of me in the doorway saying, *'I am not taking lunch today.'* I was like *'Okay, see you back in class later.'* He was looking all serious and told me, *'Today, I am fasting.'* I had no idea why he felt the need to randomly inform me of his spiritual practices, but I just said, *'Oh, that's good.'* "

"He asked me if I ever fasted too, and I was like, *'Yeah, I do occasionally. It's a great practice for gaining clarity and discipline.'* He just smiled and asked me more questions, like he was interviewing me or something".

" *'Do you have a church home?'* "

" *'How long have you been born again?'* "

" *'Is your family Christian?'* "

Ali laughed at my mimicking Benjamin's accent.

"Dar is a pretty religious city and all the Tanzanian students asked questions about our families and backgrounds as a matter of culture. I didn't mind answering."

"Finally he walked off. The next day after class he came up to me with a letter and asked me to read it later. I opened that thing up and the first lines said, *'I have come to the conclusion that you are truly born again. And our Lord has made it known to me that you are to be my wife.'* I promptly wrote him right back and said, *'God told me no such thing!'* "

Ali bent over in his chair laughing.

"You sure y'all didn't do more than study?" he asked.

I laughed, too, and brushed his joke off then went silent again, wondering how Jack got the phone number to my bungalow.

He knew exactly where I was. There was no way of getting around that fact. I think Ali could tell that I was getting upset, but he didn't ask why.

After we finished dinner, I pulled the sliced mango and papaya that I'd prepared for dessert from the fridge. I sat down on the sofa next to Ali.

"You said your mom's husband is in prison."

I blinked slowly and responded, "Yeah… You know what, I think you're kind of nosey! I've already told you waaaay too much about me. What about your background, security man? I got some questions I want to ask *you*."

"Like what?"

"What were *your* parents like?"

"My mom was a good mom— caring, hard-working, led a simple life. Like you described yours, just not as devout. She never remarried after my dad though. Had a couple of boyfriends. Didn't work out. She just did her own thing."

"Mmm hmm. So why'd you come to Bermuda?"

"I already told you why I came here. I wanted to take some time off and travel, find myself, I guess. My uncle had this house and I came here. Your story is so much more interesting than mine. I definitely haven't had an African stalker or a stepdad in prison. What's that about anyway, if you don't mind talking about it? I mean, was he another case like your dad..."

I could tell he was trying to read my face.

"Hey, if you don't wanna talk about it I understand. I don't want to pry or anything."

"What can it hurt? I thought. *"It's not like I'm going to see this guy after I leave here. Maybe sharing will help me with my writing."*

"He was actually in prison when they met."

"How the heck did that happen?!"

I suspected that Ali was making an effort to not cuss around me. I didn't think the censoring was necessary, but I appreciated the respect.

"One of my aunts introduced them. After my parents divorced, I guess my mom got lonely or bored or something. My aunt is married to this guy who was in the same prison, and they both got the bright idea to try and set this guy up with somebody. So my mom started writing him letters. She was insecure, if you ask me, and didn't pay guys on the outside any attention. She even told me that there were guys at church who seemed to like her but she couldn't believe anyone on the outside would want someone like her.

"He claims to be a reformed, jailhouse preacher. He spit some bible verses and some tired game and, boom! You gotta match made in heaven."

"Well, what is he in for?" Ali asked. "How long has he been in prison?"

"At present," I sighed, "he has served thirty-five years of a total fifty-five year sentence."

"For?"

"… for kidnapping, rape, and conspiracy."

"Whoooooa!" Ali threw up his hands and glanced back and forth as if looking for someone who'd just knocked him in the head.

"Why, wha-what?"

"Me and my brother can't figure it out either, Ali. It's nuts. We tried to talk her out of it, but it was like trying to kick through a stone wall."

"When did they get married?"

"Right before I came here."

"Ahhh… Your mom is like one of those women on those documentaries about women who marry killers. Like those women who write love letters to Charles Manson. That's Bonnie and Clyde Syndrome. You better pray for your mom."

I chose to ignore his last comment. He gave me a long sympathetic look then wrapped his arms around me in one of the most awkward, intentionally playful hugs I'd ever gotten.

"It's gonna be okay, Jane!"

I shoved him and rolled my eyes.

"That's some strange shit." he concluded. "I mean, some strange stuff."

"You know, you don't have to catch yourself when you talk to me." I said. "I've heard much worse."

"What? Oh, my language. Okay. It just seems like you're really making an effort to stay, like, positive. I don't like to do stuff to stand in people's way. I think that's a good thing."

I yawned and looked at my watch.

"It is getting pretty late, huh?" he asked.

"It's no big deal. I'm really not all that sleepy. You wanna check out this movie? It looks just as hilarious as the last one."

I didn't want to admit that I wanted him to stay longer. It was easier to pretend I wasn't exhausted. Ali nodded in agreement and plopped back down on the couch next to me— a little closer this time.

A commercial for a psychic came on. "I guess you aren't into astrology, huh?"

"I used to read my horoscope when I was little, but I don't anymore."

"Is that like, a conflict with your beliefs?"

"Kind of, if you're really taking it seriously. But I think the concept's pretty interesting, sort of entertaining."

"Yeah, I'm not really into it either, but it is kind of interesting."

He turned toward me with his arm across the back of the chair.

"Well, what's your sign?"

"Oh god, not the what's your sign question."

"Humor me."

"Leo. You?" I asked.

"Libra."

***

The movie was pretty unmemorable, but it was so much fun cracking jokes about it with Ali. We laughed halfway through it until we both fell asleep, and I woke up several hours later to an infomercial and lights that had automatically turned off by way of an energy-saving timer. He seemed to sense my movement and woke up immediately.

"What time is it?" he asked.

"A little after midnight."

"Dang, what did you put in my food? You didn't try to take advantage of me in my sleep, did you?"

"You know what, get out!"

He gave me a flirtatious wink. Then the phone rang.

"Oh, geez!" I turned to grab the phone, but Ali got to it before I could. He was like The Flash, wielding the power of super speed.

He didn't say anything right away. I smacked his arm a couple of times and tried to grab the phone while he smiled in resistance. I ran to the bedroom and picked up the other phone.

"Jane… Jane," Jack said, angrily, "I'm not gon' keep playin' this game wit you… Girl, why don't you open your mouth and say something. You picked up the phone—stop playin'!"

"Uh, yeah, man," Ali finally said, "I think you got the wrong number."

"—the hell? Who this?" Jack asked.

"I think you dialed the wrong number. Who you lookin' for?"

"Nah. Nah, brotha. I know what I dialed. Who are *you*?"

"Well… I'm Ali."

Jack paused and then laughed before answering.

"Oh, you're Ali, huh? Well, this is Jack. Pleasure to make your acquaintance."

"Okay." Ali said, seemingly thrown off by Jack's effortless code-switching.

"I'm Jane's mentor. She began working for me some time ago."

"Oh, forreal?"

Ali sounded genuinely interested. He was being sucked right in.

"That's right." Jack went on, "See, I'm a real estate developer. I rehab properties around the city, at least that's part of what I do. I also dabble in the financing end through the purchasing of notes and extension of small loans. But that's not nearly as interesting, so I won't bore you."

"Oh, okay." Ali was hanging on every word.

"Jane was assisting me with a few designs and some property-scouting for some of my biggest projects yet. She's in on some the most important redevelopment work in the city, particularly in West Philly, and I'm training her closely in my area of expertise."

"Oh wow," Ali said, "she hadn't mentioned anything about that."

"Okay." Jack said.

I just knew that he wanted to find out how much I had mentioned to Ali, how much time we'd spent together.

"Well, I don't know what she *has* mentioned to you about us, but she is pretty integral to the work I'm doing here. You could say she's… my most important investment."

"Oh, okay." Ali said.

"…Anyway, it was cool meeting you, man. You seem like an okay dude. I mean, what, y'all havin' a lil' get together round there or something? I hear some music in the background."

I put the phone down on the bed and ran into the hallway where Ali could see me motion vigorously for him to zip his lips. As comfortable as he was, he was bound to say too much.

Ali stammered for a second then said, "Uh, yeah. Well, we just chillin', man, you know. B-but it's getting pretty late round here. I don't know your time there, but it's getting pretty late here, in Bermuda. I was actually just bout to leave."

"Yeah… okay." Jack said sounding suspicious. "Well, when the get together is over tell her to give me a call."

"Oh, no problem. Will do!" Ali said with the enthusiasm of a well-trained butler. I couldn't believe him.

"I 'preciate that." Jack said. "Just wanna make sure she's alright, you know. School starting up again soon. Gotta keep her on track. You understand."

"Yeah, straight up. It was nice meeting you."

"Yeah, you too… Ali."

Ali hung up the phone and casually walked over to the kitchen for a bottle of water.

"He seemed cool. Why don't you want to talk to him?"

"He's not as cool as you think," I said. "and you're just being nosey!"

As I walked back toward the couch, that big floral arrangement I got caught my eye.

"Why do you say that?" Ali asked.

I realized that the delivery slip did not convey any information about an international order. Of course, there was no sender information, but I had expected there to be some indication of the country of origin for the order.

"Is he really the reason you came here?" Ali asked while my mind ticked with questions about the flowers.

I finally responded, "Partly."

I guess I was starting to look particularly worried, because he put down the bottle and walked slowly toward me.

"Well, the caller ID showed a US number."

"Yeah, but it wasn't his number. He was using another phone. And he could have spoofed the number."

I remembered being in one of my meetings with Jack where he called another real estate investor to get information about a property on the sneak. He knew this guy wouldn't be forthcoming if he knew Jack was another investor attempting to purchase the same property. So he used a spoofed number and pretended to be a potential renter.

"Remember the cave? Maybe he's here."

"Come on, Jane. You sure about that?" Ali asked.

"Why is he being all incognito?" I asked, almost to myself. "I just came here because I needed a break, from all of this. Why is he being sneaky? Oh my God, if he's here…"

I buried my face in my hands, and Ali put his arm around my shoulder gently.

"Well, I guess I'm spending the night after all."

He walked back out into the living room and stretched out unabashedly on the couch as I looked on.

"I doubt it's all that serious." Ali said with a lighthearted grin. But if it makes you feel any better, ya got company."

I hesitated then flopped down next to him. As if trying to erase the strangeness in the air and create the perfect ending to the evening, I regrouped and said,

"You know, you can stay if you want."

"Okay."

"No, really." I insisted, wanting him to play along at least a little and act as if he'd been invited to stay. "You're not imposing. I'm really enjoying your company."

"Okay. That's what I said."

He leaned across me for the remote, turned off the TV and, paused. The soft kiss he gave me lingered even after his lips left me.

I rested my head on his chest and said, "You forgot to open the shades."

18

I stood at the entrance to Admiral's cave alone and looked down. A full moon shined above. The sinkhole was filled to the top with water. In it, my reflection was cool, expressionless. Spellbound, I barely moved. Then, as if taken over by some force outside myself, I jumped in.

I spiraled down for what felt like miles, past layers of craggy earth, landing in some hidden chamber. Out of nowhere, a tall, shrouded figure with red eyes and a flowing, hooded black gown rushed toward me. I could not run.

He pushed me with a force that knocked the wind right out of me and sent me spiraling further into the darkness. I landed again in another chamber. It had the typical interior of so many of the bungalows on the island, but its walls were all limestone rock. Beautiful paintings and sculptures complimented the furniture and the walls. From outside myself, I could see Ali and I casually watching TV, then me walking toward the bedroom in my pajamas.

I tumbled further into a room filled with rolled up architectural plans and old school drafting tables where men and women sat hunched over, feverishly working.

I looked out a porthole in the rock wall and saw a plane take off while I stood on the tarmac waving. The ground then crumbled beneath my feet and I was falling once more.

I flailed my arms and legs, as if trying to force solid earth to reappear beneath me and restore my sense of groundedness. Then I looked to my left and saw what looked like Jack falling alongside me. His body picked up speed and was out of sight in an instant, while mine came to a stop and hovered in the cavern.

Suddenly, I was moving in reverse, flying upward and beginning to awaken from my numb state. Light from above became visible, and I gasped for air just as my head surfaced at the top of the sinkhole.

I woke up shaken and emotional. It was like I hadn't slept at all. I made a mental note of the key elements of the dream. Then, in the dark, I patted myself down frantically and was terrified to find that I had indeed removed my shirt in my sleep.

"What the hell is WRONG with you? Jesus, Ali, don't wake up, DO NOT wake up!"

I looked to my right. Ali was sleeping peacefully with my shirt lying on top of his right hand. To create as little a disturbance as possible, I'd have to stay seated next to him, reach across him, and get my shirt. Then I'd have to put it back on, all while not waking him up.

"You could just grab the shirt and make a run for it to your room! By the time he wakes up you'll be gone."

I wasn't sure if that would work, and I was too afraid to move that much. I leaned forward gingerly, taking cues from one of those slow-moving sloths from that zoo commercial a few hours ago. I could feel his breath on my neck change pace the moment I grasped the corner of my sleeve.

"Do not… move… again."

I waited… and waited for him to settle back into a deep sleep while holding a position similar to the warrior pose I learned from a free yoga video online. My shoulder started to burn, and trembling could have set in if he didn't start snoring right after that. I knew it was safe to grab the shirt and slide it back on.

I drank some water and went back to sleep, relieved that fate had not betrayed me again with the ultimate embarrassment.

***

At seven twenty that morning, I got up and went into the bedroom for my morning devotion. Ali got up at eight and found me quietly studying.

"What are you reading?"

"It's a devotional book. Helps me get in the right frame of mind for the day."

"You read that every morning?"

"Try to. Luckily, this morning, I'm wide awake and not nodding off. That can really be a struggle some days."

Ali stood in the doorway silently looking at me.

"Why you lookin' like that?" he asked.

"Like what?"

"Why you got your bottom lip all poked out like you're sad or something?"

"Huh?" I sat up and looked in the mirror to see what he was talking about.

"What? I look normal."

"Oh, my bad. You just got a pouty bottom lip. Well, pick it up then." He poked at my side to tickle me. Then he asked, "You still worried about Jack?"

The mention of that name threatened to jolt me out of my sense of peace, so I quickly changed the subject.

"Don't you have to work today?" I said, swatting at his hands.

"Yeah, later. But I need go to my place, shower and what not."

Having breakfast and spending the morning together seemed like the most natural next thing, but I didn't want to ask for too much of his time. I had already given the impression of being needy enough. I didn't also want to be clingy.

"Okay." I said.

"So, what you trying to do today? You still haven't checked out Hamilton Parish or Historic St. George, right?"

"No, I haven't."

"We can go to one of those places."

I was elated by the fact that spending time together seemed just as natural to him as it did to me. He said it so plainly, as if we'd flown to Bermuda together and were just checking the next thing off the itinerary.

"Sounds good." I said with a smile that was broadening with each passing second. "I'll call you when I'm dressed and ready."

On the bus to Historic St. George I silently stared out the window, absorbing the scenery and letting my mind take a break from planning and analyzing. Ali pinched my arm with the hand that was resting around my waist.

"You're pretty quiet all of a sudden."

I smirked and shrugged my shoulders. He smiled knowingly.

"You're not going back, are you?"

I stared at the seat in front of me, then looked back out the window.

"That's exactly how it happened with me. Said I was just coming out here for a visit, to clear my head. Then I got a little sun, hung out at the beach, walked the trail a couple of times, and that was it. It just wasn't worth going back."

"You said before that you wanted to stay out of trouble. Now you're talkin' about having to clear your head. What's up, Ali? What did you leave in Maryland?"

"It's not that big a thing. I was just a confused kid."

"Come on, there's nothing sensational in your history? Don't let me feel like I'm the only one with crazy in the closet."

"It really wasn't all that complicated. I was in school. Mom was working and paying my tuition. Then she got laid off and couldn't keep paying the bills. I was already working but couldn't put in a lot of hours because of classes. So I started looking for ways to make some extra money."

"Supplemental income," I said.

"Yeah, something like that. You know how it is on college campuses. A lot of people always looking for the next party, the next release. I just saw it as an opportunity then."

"Okaaaay."

I looked back out the window hoping that he wouldn't recognize the slight look of surprise on my face. A drug dealer? I had come all this way to escape the criminal element. And he seemed like such a wonderful, happy-go-lucky guy. The thought made me uneasy, but I calmed my fears by choosing to trust that he'd closed that chapter of his life when he moved to Bermuda.

He stared at me then changed the subject.

"If you stay, you're gonna need to find a job."

"Yeah, I've been thinking about that. But I've done some of the research, and it looks like I would need a work permit."

"Yep, and the permit has to come from your prospective employer, so we have to find you a job first."

"We?"

"You know of any places I can look into? I have some money in the bank for now, but I'll need work at least until the start of the summer semester."

Placing a timeline on my stay gave me a sense of purpose, but also sadness in knowing that my time with Ali would be limited. Four and a half months seemed like a good chunk of time but wouldn't be nearly enough for what was sparking between us. I think he got a sense of that same sadness, because he pulled me in closer.

"Tell me what kind of experience you have so I'll know which of my contacts to check with."

"Most of my experience is clerical. I've been doing secretarial jobs pretty much since right after high school. But I've also been a nanny, a record keeper at this historic house museum, a telemarketer, sold knives once, done retail. I briefly had a paper route, but who reads papers anymore? I've worked in food service, did a tiny bit of modeling. Oh, and I do hair on the side. But I think the clerical experience would probably be the most applicable because it's the most long-standing and extensive."

"Damn. That's a lot of jobs." he said.

"I've done most of that stuff since I moved to Philly. Takes a few jobs or side jobs to keep things rolling. Hey, if you know anybody in the design or construction area, that would be awesome."

"I'll call some people this afternoon. Not sure if they'll know anyone working in your field, but I know I can find you something. Oh wait..." Ali sat back in his chair and rubbed his chin.

"What is it?"

He bit his lip like people do when they need to say something that may not be welcome news.

"You don't have right of residency, so trying to stay here long term could become complicated."

"I already thought that out. I made an appointment with Immigration to extend my visit, and I'm hoping to get things in line in the meantime..." I looked at him, still gauging his interest. "... with your help. It means I need to find a job really quick."

"The job's done. I just have to ask around to find the best fit for you. But with housing, that's trickier in terms of timing. When it comes to finding a place, the easiest place to get would be in something like a boarding house."

"That's what I was thinking."

"But the owners of some of these boarding houses cater to tourists, and they don't really check backgrounds and papers. Those are probably not the kinds of places you want to be in long term."

"And then, what if I still can't get residency in time?"

He tapped on his temple then smiled as if he knew the answer all along.

"Girl, you can stay with me! You can get by if you cohabit with a resident."

I was thinking that, and hoping he was thinking that, but didn't want to let on that I wanted that. I knew how uncomfortable living with other people had been for me in the past, and I didn't want to establish what felt like such a significant dependency on any man, especially him. Plus, I was supposed to be trying to take things slowly.

"Well, let's see what comes through, first." I said.

His smile waned a little and he looked somewhat disappointed to hear my response, but he seemed to make a conscious effort to remain upbeat.

"Cool."

***

After another amazing day with Ali, I returned to my bungalow and called Devi for a talk that was long overdue. I laid all my journals out on the bed along with the dreams I'd recorded and the nearly empty notebook I'd brought for reflecting during my trip.

"Hi, Jane. How's everything been?"

"Still going very well. I feel so relaxed and hopeful. It's been a long time since I've felt this happy. But then, I guess that's because I don't have many responsibilities here. I can't expect that to last, right?"

"I didn't say that. If you're happy there, what does that tell you?"

"... That maybe the way I've been going about all this is too intense."

"Riiii-ight!"

"I know, I know. I've always been too hard on myself, too intense. But there's so much I need to get done!"

"Yeah, and we gotta figure out why that is. Look, don't assume you have to be miserable in order to be responsible. Happiness is not something bad. It is a choice and has to be cultivated like any other character trait so that you can be balanced."

"Okay... so then, now I don't feel so guilty for making the decision I made."

"What decision?"

"I'm taking the semester off."

"Thank God!"

I was a little surprised by her reaction.

"I was afraid you were headed for a nervous breakdown." she said.

"You and my mom were. I'm gonna get a job here and stay for a while. I researched this boarding house online that seems really quiet, and I think it'll be the perfect environment."

"Alright, now are you sure you want to spend that much time in a place with people always going in and out? I know how you are about your living space."

"Well it only has four rooms, and it's not like a college dorm with people being loud, punching holes in walls and blasting music all the time."

"Yeah, but what kinds of people are these other boarders? Transients? You have to be careful, Jane. Did you see any other affordable options that would be safer?"

"I'm still doing some research. There's a lot out there, and much of it is priced well. So I'm sure I'll find something soon. I just really liked the location and the style of this one. It's a beautiful Bermuda Style home on a hill overlooking a bay. I'll ask a friend to go with me, to ride over there to get a look and talk to the owner."

"Oh, a friend, huh? Is he the one who gave you the flowers?"

"Hey, how do you know it's a man?!"

"Girl, please. Who is he?"

"His name's Ali. He's a security guard here at the resort and he does tours around the islands. He showed me around a few places. He's also a sculptor. We've just been hanging out."

Though I tried to downplay my giddiness, I'm sure she heard the smile on my face.

"Are you taking your time?"

"Trying to." I said, with a bit of uncertainty.

"Well, let's get back to the last thing we talked about before you left. How's the assignment coming?"

"Yeah… so… I've been recording a few really interesting dreams I've had, which I think will be pretty revealing. My subconscious is trying to work something out. And I've read over some of my past journal entries to analyze what I was thinking then and how that contributed to what I experienced. I was thinking about some of the men I dated and why I was attracted to them. Like Kobina— you remember, Kobina— and how he was married. I was totally clueless. And then there was Maxwell before that—"

"You haven't written a thing, have you?"

I was quiet for a moment. She could always sniff me out.

"Nothing except the dream recordings." I said sheepishly.

"Yeah, soon as you started getting into all of that *'I read through my journals,'* I knew you hadn't written anything. It's okay. Just say, *'Well, Devi, I didn't write anything.'* "

Devi had a moment poking fun at me the way she always did when I tried to talk around her questions.

"Okay, well, during your time with Ali, have you noticed anything different about your experience with him? Does the way you feel, the way you act with him, differ than with previous men?"

I thought for a moment and said, "I do feel a lot more comfortable with him. He's really easy-going. Always has a smile on his face. I don't feel tense at all around him. He has a very accepting nature."

"Accepting. What do you mean by that?"

"We talked about our pasts a little, and he doesn't seem put off by mine. He doesn't seem put off by me in general. And he's three years younger than me. I'm so used to guys in my age range refusing to approach me because, supposedly, I'm intense."

"Yes, you are intense." Devi was sure to add. "Go on."

"And… I'm having a hard time describing the feeling… but it's just this sense of satisfaction, this sense of fullness I get whenever he comes around. I want him to come by or call, and he does. So far, I haven't had to wait around wondering what he thinks of me. I don't have to hurry up and wipe the hope of spending time with him out of my mind, because he always shows up. It just proves that he feels exactly the way I feel."

"Hmm. And how do you think a good experience like this could be possible? Does it have to do with the environment? How have your feelings played into it?"

"My feelings. You mean about men?"

"I mean your current emotional state. The feelings produced by leaving school, and Philadelphia, and all that drama, to get some peace."

"Oh. Well, I feel more open. Because I'm a lot more relaxed. I don't feel so guarded. I didn't have any particular expectations of what I would experience here. I just looked forward to having a good time and enjoyed what came."

"See what a less hectic life can get ya? I bet you're not even grinding your teeth in your sleep, are you?"

I checked the insides of my cheeks for those telltale ridges that my teeth had been leaving behind for the past couple of years.

"Nope!"

"And," Devi asked, "no more nightmares about being shot at point blank range indicating the extent to which you feel like you're facing inescapable stress?"

"Right."

"I'm not saying you should leave everything behind for good. But restructuring some things so that you can have a more peaceful existence is something you should seriously consider. And it's not about Ali, either. It's about your own agency. Taking control over your own well-being. See Jane, the assignment would have been one way for you to gain perspective. But I think the Spirit had other plans. Experience can often be the best teacher. I trust that you'll keep your eyes and ears, your mind and your heart open. I still would suggest you write if you feel the need, but most importantly, continue to be observant. OK?"

"OK."

"And don't go making a psychiatrist out of that man. Just have fun, alright? Whatever you've told him, don't tell him anymore until some time passes, okay?"

Though I'd already given Ali a laundry list of my issues, I could still think of some key items that had not yet been revealed.

"OK."

19

The next morning, I got a return phone call from my brother, Terrence. He was the first person I wanted to tell that I was taking time off from school, but he wasn't at home when I'd called him the night before."

"What up, sis! How's island life?"

"Gorgeous! A thousand times more than what I hoped for. How's everything with you? How's Vonnie?"

"Mom's good. I'm good. Just got word yesterday that they might need some guys for a project in Washington state, so looks like I'll be traveling soon myself."

"Sounds good. How long will the project be?"

"Couple of months."

"Wow."

"Yeah. You know I'm always on the lookout for those international projects. Get some more stamps on that passport. But this'll do just fine."

"Yeah, man. Get that travel under your belt. That's always good. And speaking of that, I called to tell you that I decided to extend my trip, just for a short while. I have some job prospects and I'm looking at a few places."

"Why did I know that was coming?" Terrence asked.

"Well, y'all know holding everything together in Philly has been a challenge. I'm still doing okay, but I just want to slow down a little, get some rest."

"Look, you don't have to explain anything to me. I know you got this."

"I know Ma is gonna be worried about me being out here alone. I was planning to call her later today after she wakes up from her nap."

"Well, that's Mom. But I gotta tell you, Jane, she's come a long way from that Virginia Tech incident. She's proud of what you've done, and she trusts you to make the right decision. And she knew you needed a break. She was round here worrying about how much weight you lost."

"I tried to tell her I lost that weight from working out. It helps with the stress."

"Don't make no difference to her. She was talking 'bout how you was losing all the lil' bit of tail you had."

I burst out laughing and remembered her teasing me during Christmas break in her Grandma Sadie voice: *"You still got a lil' bit o' tail left. Don't lose it all. You know us women 'sposed to have some tail!"*

I weighed one hundred and forty pounds at five feet, eight inches. I'd only lost five pounds, but it was enough to make my pants look just a little looser. A few pounds more, and I'm sure my mom would have been praying away the anorexic demon.

"That's Vonnie! I know she's just looking out for me."

"Always," Terrence said.

"And I appreciate how you've looked out for me, too."

"Oh, stop it." he said.

"Your support is very much appreciated, and you know I'll always be grateful for you helping to pay my tuition my first year. There aren't a lot of siblings out there who have what we have, and I'll always be thankful for that."

"If I have it, you got it. That's how we roll." he said. "I wasn't going let you miss out again. I know you'd do the same for me."

As I wrapped up my conversation with Terrence, I went to the door to get a feel for the temperature. I noticed a letter in my mailbox and took it out.

Just as I was opening it, my cell phone rang again.

"Jane, your light bill is gonna be high as hell this month, and you can't blame me!" Celine yelled on the other end.

"Well, greetings to you, too." I said. "What are you talking about?"

"I went by to move in some stuff, and saw that you left the kitchen and the bedroom light on!"

"No the hell I didn't!"

"They were *on*! You couldn't wait to get away, could you?"

"Celine, I know for a fact that I didn't leave anything on. I specifically remember checking and double checking before I left. Then my landlord sent maintenance there a couple of days ago to check on the place, because my neighbor was complaining about some noise that they thought was coming from my heating system or something. I'm sure they wouldn't have left— wait a minute, wait."

"What, what!" Celine pushed me for an answer as a horrific explanation for Jack's recent behavior began to take shape in my mind.

"Did anything look like it was out of place?" I asked.

"Out of place? No. Your place was immaculate as usual. Except for a bunch of papers around your desk. Looked like some had fallen on the floor."

"That was probably the information that I left on my desk for you, the resort information, so you'd know where I am."

"Yeah, I saw it all. Everything else looked fine, Jane. But if you're concerned about somebody being in your place why don't you just check the footage from your camera. I didn't know ya had one, but that was a pretty smart move. Leave it to you!"

"A camera? What camera?"

"Jane," Celine said, calling me back as if I'd wandered off into some distant place. "There's a camera in your apartment, sitting right on top of the harp of your living room lamp. You didn't put it there?"

She must have known I was stunned and terrified, because she switched from attempting to remind me to giving me as much detail as possible.

"It's a tiny little camera. I wouldn't have noticed it myself except that my heel got caught in the carpet and I almost tripped and knocked the lamp over on the way out. That's when I saw it. It's a tiny little thing, like the ones we used for the model cams in that fashion expo last Spring."

"It's Jack," I said, with tears welling up in my eyes. "Do not go back there, okay? You gotta get the cops over there. I'll call and see what I can do from my end. Let them know that you're housesitting for me and you suspect that someone broke in. Tell them it was Jack."

Celine agreed.

Right after she hung up I started attempting to put the sequence of events together in my head. If Jack was just in my apartment two days ago, he must not have been in Bermuda when he called my bungalow. But why would he put a camera in my place after I'd already left town?

"Maybe he didn't. Maybe he planted it before."

That could explain the strange noises my neighbor had complained about. I sat on the couch for several minutes trying to figure out what to do and praying that Jack was still playing spy in Philadelphia where the police could nab him.

There was a knock at the door. I nearly jumped out of my skin. After dropping the envelope to the floor, the contents of which I still hadn't viewed, I looked at the door in astonishment. I got up the courage to peek out the window and saw Ali standing outside then breathed a sigh of relief.

There was no way I was going to dump this on him. As long as Jack was still back home, I'd continue with my plans and not burden Ali with any more of my drama. With Celine's help, and a little— no a lot— of prayer, I'd solve this thing and get on with my life. I opened the door.

"You ready for work?" he asked as we enjoyed a long embrace.

"What?"

"Talked to one of the tour specialists I work for and he told me a spot just opened up for an arborist's assistant at the Arboretum. It's in Devonshire, close to Hamilton Parish."

I jumped up wrapping my arms around his neck and gave him a kiss that started off friendly but slowly turned into something else. We quickly parted and I turned my head slightly. I did a mental check to keep the surges of pleasure at bay. Ali continued talking but was clearly thrown off guard.

"There's some office work involved— keeping records and dealing with some contractors. But you get to work around the grounds too. I know you said you didn't want gardening to become a chore, but it sounds like a good gig."

"This is awesome! Thank you so much. Now I see how simple life can be when I stop complicating everything. What time do I have to be there? I mean, this is like an interview, right?"

"It's supposed to be an interview, but I doubt they'll take you through a bunch of changes. They haven't had much interest in the position at all and they need to get ready for the high season. You better go ahead and change clothes. You gotta be there in an hour."

"What?! Ali, why didn't you call me? I could've been getting ready all this time." I snatched off my shoes and started toward the bedroom to change. "I gotta print out a copy of my resume."

He stood there watching me, a large grin on his face. "I'm just playing!" he said. "You don't have to be there 'til tomorrow morning at nine thirty."

I sighed and threw one of my sandals at him.

***

Ali was right about the job. When I arrived at nine fifteen for the appointment, the arborist looked me up and down. He complimented my jacket, asked me a few questions and gave me khaki pants, a green polo shirt and boots to change into. Both my work permit and residency status were granted in an unusually short amount of time, all thanks to Ali's connections.

The only problem left was finding a place I could afford. The arborist assistant position paid enough to allow me to stay at the boarding house of my choice. But it was all booked up by the time my residency status was granted. I quickly learned that other places were also in high demand leaving only a few undesirables with shady owners and boarders, poorly maintained properties, and plenty of vacancies.

I had truly come to love my little vacation spot in Jobson's Cove, and I knew that when the tourist season heated up that area would remain relatively quiet. It was also a plus that Ali's place was only a ten minute walk away.

I gradually began to lose sight of what had happened in my apartment in Philly, mostly by choice. The police were slow to respond to Celine's call and still hadn't come to any conclusions about the break in. There were no more phone calls from Jack. I stopped checking my email.

Maybe the police had at least contacted Jack and the investigation caused him to lay low. I told myself that God would handle it and preferred to cling to my newfound sense of peace.

The day before my stay at the resort was set to expire, I had a decision to make. There was still plenty of money in my bank account to get me through my semester off in Bermuda. Did I really want to spend all of that man's money, though? Technically it was mine, but using it could certainly mean that I would be that much more indebted to him.

"Oh, what does it matter. He already thinks you belong to him— money or no money. Not spending it won't change a thing."

I had paid about $840 a week for my vacation in the bungalow plus $800 for my plane ticket and expenses. An extended stay option at the resort would provide a twenty percent discount which would bring my weekly rate down to $672. If I gave myself an ample six weeks to find a decent, more permanent place, it would cost me $4032 to stay in the bungalow in the meantime. I'd still have more than $3000 left over. Plus I was working, so I could just stash the rest of Jack's money as a cushion.

***

The next two weeks were sublime. I came home every day after work feeling refreshed after spending the afternoons in the sun and among the trees at the arboretum. I took a swim in the pool and had dinner with Ali.

We initially agreed to take turns making dinner, but after one night of burnt hot dogs and spaghetti at his place, I didn't mind taking on most of the cooking. Every Friday, he took me to a new restaurant on the island.

One evening as he was walking me back to the resort we noticed a small crowd of onlookers peeking around maintenance workers, security guards and police officers hovering over something on my patio.

When we broke through the crowd, we saw Ali's neighbor's dog lying motionless next to a chewed up rope toy by the back door.

"Pops!" Ali gasped.

I covered my mouth in shock.

Mr. Clayton saw us and came rushing over to meet us.

"Ay, Ali! Uh, hello, young lady." This time, the look on his face was one of concern rather than curiosity.

"Mr. Clayton," I said, "what happened? How did the dog even get here."

"Poor lil' fella must've had an amazing memory. Looks like he was just playing with that rope and probably rubbed it in some of that stuff they put down to keep the bugs away. I was going for a walk and saw him lying back here. Your gate was *wide open,*" he said in a quite accusatory tone.

Ali glanced at me, looking worried, then asked Mr. Clayton, "Was there anything else strange?"

He took a deep breath and looked at both of us before saying, "Well, what made me come back here in the first place was some man I saw walking around near the gate. It was one of them bums that come roaming around the beaches sometimes. I didn't know what he was doing 'til I saw the dog and figured he was probably trying to see if it was alright."

"Did you say anything to him?" Ali asked.

"Naw! I don't mess with these crazy folks that get to walking around on these beaches. I just called security."

I went over to meet the police at my patio door. As I walked away, I could hear Mr. Clayton say to Ali,

"You know what that man was here for."

"Mr. Clayton, you know I can hear you!" I yelled back.

"And folks can SEE you!" he retorted.

"Dirty old man!"

Ali sucked his teeth and said, "Thanks, Mr. Clayton" in a tone that didn't sound very grateful.

One of the police officers told me, "It appears to have all been accidental. Maintenance says they just sprayed for bugs and the little guy might have gotten his toy into a very saturated area."

"What about the man Mr. Clayton says he saw, the one who was by my gate?"

"We have someone looking for him. He may have been intoxicated. A lot of these beach people are heavy drinkers. But I can assure you, this is an isolated incident. We haven't had reports of one of them coming around here for months. When they do come around, they're just looking for a quiet beach to crash on for the night. He may have even just wanted to play with the dog. Sometimes stray animals are the only company those people get in a day. We'll keep you informed of our findings."

Ali talked to a couple of the security guards and joined me at my back door as the cops left and the crowd dispersed.

"These guys don't know anything. They haven't dealt with any trespassers recently and said none of the other guests saw anything."

"Oh my God, Ali. Ask Mr. Clayton what the guy looked like."

Ali walked back over to Mr. Clayton's yard and asked for a description of the trespasser.

"He was a trim guy, but pretty tall, about your height, I guess. He had on a hat and a long coat, bunch of scraggly layers— the usual bum getup. I didn't get a good look at his face, but he was black."

"Thanks, Mr. Clayton."

We walked toward my front door and Ali said to me,

"Look, Jane. I know this was probably just another random crazy thing that happened, but I don't feel right leaving you. I'm not comfortable with you staying here by yourself tonight. You can stay at my place or I can stay with you here."

"Don't you have to work?"

"I took the night off."

"I'd rather we stay here."

While Ali watched TV in the living room, I took a long, hot shower. I was relieved to know that the trespasser was pretty tall. That meant he didn't quite fit Jack's description. I trusted that Pops' death had indeed been a random, isolated incident. Still, I was uneasy.

I reached for a new bottle of coconut milk shampoo and started washing my hair when Ali banged on the bathroom door.

"Jane!"

"What?!"

He opened the bathroom door and walked in.

"Jane?"

"I'm in the shower! You can't just walk in here like that."

"Why didn't you tell me about this?"

I peeked around the shower curtain, squinting through soapy water, and saw him holding emails that I'd printed about the break-in investigation and the envelope with the contents that I had completely forgotten to examine.

"This was on your table."

"Why the heck were you poking around in my mail?"

"Why didn't you tell me about this?"

"You're upset about Pops. Just try to relax and forget about messing around in my stuff!"

"That's not what I asked you! This is some crazy shit."

"Can I get the shampoo out of my hair and put some clothes on first, please?"

He left the bathroom, and I finished up in the shower. I stalled a few more minutes by making tea in the kitchen then went into the bedroom. He was already there, sitting on the floor in front of the bed, scratching his head.

"I don't want to scare you," he said, "but I'm starting to think some of this stuff is connected. The phone calls, Pops, whoever that was at the cave, this stuff."

"Yeah but with the stuff happening all the way back in Philly, there's no way he's here."

"I don't get it." Ali was rubbing his eyes, looking partly confused and partly fatigued.

"You still haven't told me what's really up with this guy. I mean, what kind of mentor acts the way he did? When you talked to him, it definitely sounded like there was more to it than that."

I looked away from Ali and shook my head, unable to think of a good reason for keeping my dealings with Jack a secret.

"You don't think there's anything else I need to know?" He asked.

I didn't answer.

He stood up, dropped the contents of the envelope on the bed, then started poking around in my closet and under my bed. Contained in the envelope were photographs of me leaving my apartment, going to the ATM, and boarding the plane at the Philadelphia International Airport.

"See," I said brushing aside the fear that could have set in, "these photos were all taken in Philly. I'm almost sure the investigation into the break-in stopped him in his tracks… Why are you going through my stuff?!"

He only responded, "Uhh huh."

After finding my suitcases, he pulled them out and opened them.

"What are you doing?" I asked.

"Helping you pack."

"Wait a minute!"

"I don't know why you went through all that immigration shit just so you wouldn't have to move in with me. You wanna take care of yourself, I get it. But you're not staying here by yourself anymore. First thing in the morning, we're checking out of here and going to the police station. Then you're coming to my place."

He emptied out one of my drawers then paused before fully opening the one with my underclothes.

"Take care of that."

He pointed to the drawer that I was instructed to clear out and walked into the kitchen to empty the cabinets. When he was done he laid down next to me without saying a word.

"Is your place clean?" I asked.

"Your room is. The rest of the place isn't bad, I just cleaned this week."

"*This* week? You mean you don't clean *every* week? What about the second bathroom?"

He glared at me in annoyance.

Each time I had dinner at Ali's place, I was comfortable there. It was still decorated with a lot of the traditional furniture that his late uncle left behind along with Ali's sculptures. I actually liked his place, and I was glad to see he wasn't a slob.

But it was still a man's house. And I hated dirty bathrooms, which my other boyfriends had. If I saw a few stray hairs on the bathroom floor I was likely to be peeved. I knew my need for a pristine environment would spoil my ability to enjoy myself if I was presented with any form of filth in my room my first day there.

I was distracting myself by worrying about the cleanliness of Ali's house.

Also, this was only Ali's second time spending the night in my place. I could hold out for a while sleeping in my own room, but I knew that at some point we'd be watching a movie or talking late at night and end up in the same bed… in his house… and I'd have nowhere else to go but to the next room.

And the fact that I'd be paying him significantly lower rent meant that I'd save a lot of money and could possibly stay longer. How long could either of us disregard the sexual tension?

***

As we got ready to leave my bungalow the next morning, I came clean to Ali.

"I thought about what you said last night, and I'm sorry for not telling you about everything. And I appreciate all that you've done and what you're doing to help me. I'm totally okay with going to the police and at least making them aware of what's been happening."

"Yep. Just as soon as you check out of here."

"But checkout isn't required until ten. Don't you think we should go to the police station first?"

"It's only gonna take a few minutes for you to check out."

We grabbed my stuff and he rolled my suitcases down to reception. Then he stood at the door with his arms folded as I checked out.

At the police station, we described our experiences to one of the same officers who was at my bungalow the night before. There was no way for them to know if all the events we described were connected, and they didn't have enough evidence to warrant a deeper investigation. We just had to wait and see what happened next and call for help if there was a real threat.

20

"Ouch!"

I'd bumped my toe on a chair as I walked across the room to open the window. It was unseasonably warm during my first week at Ali's, and I had undressed again in my sleep.

As I fumbled around in the dark for my nightie, the bedroom door flew open. Ali turned on the light.

"No!" I screamed.

"What are you doing in here?" Ali asked, looking at me as if the fact that I was naked was not apparent.

"I opened a window." I said covering up with the nightie.

"Oh, I heard something. I was just checking… I see you're feeling comfortable."

"Why are you still looking at me?!"

He turned around and stood in the doorway facing the hallway.

"You don't know how to knock?" I asked, livid.

"Why would I automatically think to knock on a door in my own house?! It's a force of habit, alright. Sorry."

"Well, common sense should kick in and tell you that there's now a woman in your house, and you probably shouldn't go busting doors open without knocking."

I briefly thought to warn him about my nocturnal mishaps, but I decided not to give him another reason to *forget* to knock.

"Why didn't you just lock it?" he asked.

"I… forgot."

"Anyway," he said, "I already know you be walking around in here free as a bird when I'm at work."

"You saw me?!"

"Nope, I was lying, but now I know you do!"

He laughed as he walked back down the hallway to his room.

I yelled after him, "Don't think you're being slick." Although I couldn't help but to smile even as I slammed and locked the door.

He taunted me from his room, "Pick up your lip and go back to sleep!"

***

Over the next couple of days, I thought about how inconsistent I had been in my spiritual practice during my stay. The temptation to sleep in rather than getting up at 6 a.m. to pray was overwhelming, since sleep had become such a valuable commodity for me over the last few years. I was still making time for devotion, though, squeezing it in after lunch or at night before bed.

However, I had not been to church, and nothing could replace that boost I got in a spirited prayer or praise and worship service. It was part of what I needed to feel centered again. I did some research and decided to visit the Evangelical Friends Church of Bermuda that following Sunday.

After one Sunday service and Wednesday night bible study, I was hooked. I felt connected and spiritually full and prepared to face anything that would come my way.

I had extra time on my hands, and I wanted to contribute something to the assembly that was becoming my temporary church home. So, one Sunday afternoon, I volunteered to help with a youth awards ceremony. We were celebrating the academic achievements of the church's teens and encouraging them to finish the year strong.

Along with two other young volunteers, I stood at the front of the sanctuary in an elegant, pale yellow, pencil skirt with matching top, head wrap and sandals. The pastor gave a stirring introduction then we, the volunteers, stepped forward to hand out the awards.

As the Pastor gathered up his papers to start calling out names, one of the church's members, Brother Simon, jogged up to the place where we were standing and said in my ear,

"You look better than Vanna White up here!"

"Okay, Brother Simon," the Pastor remarked, signaling for him to sit down promptly. Then he began calling the students up one by one.

I got distracted when a tall man in a hat and gray trench coat quietly entered the sanctuary and sat on the back row. He kept his head down at first, then looked slowly around the sanctuary and settled his eyes squarely on me. His face was a bit dirty, and since he was so far away, I couldn't make out any distinctive features. When all the students had been called, I looked back to the place where he sat, but he was gone.

"I am sure glad you decided to make this your place of worship while you're here, Sister Jane." Brother Simon had made himself welcome to a seat next to me at the dinner that followed the awards ceremony.

"This is a very welcoming congregation." I responded politely.

Brother Simon was always a gentleman, even if he was a bit enthusiastic. He was the only man in the congregation to take in interest in me, and I was glad that he posed no threat of temptation whatsoever. He was nearly twice my age and looked it. I could hear the outcome of his earlier boxing career in the slight slurring of his words.

"That's what we got to do," he said, "show the love of the Lord and be friendly! Didn't you say you're from Philly? I have some friends there. You know the Conyers?"

"I'm sorry, I don't think I do."

"They're Episcopalian. Have you been to any Episcopal churches in Philly?"

"No." I said, trying to swallow a fork full of chicken. "I go to a church like this one, non-denominational."

"So what school do you attend?"

I started to answer the question then rushed to get the Pastor's attention once I saw that he had a free moment. As nice as he was, it was a relief having a legitimate reason for breaking away from Brother Simon.

"Pastor Hayward. I don't want to butt in too much on your dinner but I have a question for you."

"Oh, it's no problem at all. What is it, Jane."

"Was the church's food pantry open today during the same time as the ceremony? I saw someone come in who looked like he may have been homeless."

"No, the pantry's not open on Sunday afternoons, only weekdays. I did see that gentleman, though, the one on the very back row in the gray coat?"

"Yes. Did he look familiar to you at all? I thought maybe he was hoping for a meal after service."

"No, I didn't recognize him. He did leave in a flash. Hopefully he at least got something out of the prayer. He may be back in his own time."

"Of course."

At that moment, I thought about calling Ali or asking one of the members for a ride home. But the church was within walking distance of Ali's place, and I hated the feeling of living in fear. It was a bright, beautiful evening with the sun leaving fiery magenta and yellow ribbons across the sky as it set and the bay heaving in anticipation of who knew what. I wanted to continue feeling alive and satiated in my own skin, to take in the warm ocean breezes and invite whatever awaited me, whatever awaited us.

I walked home, carefully observing the forms and faces of each person I passed on the way. When I arrived, I was surprised to find Ali there.

"Don't you have to work this evening?"

"No, I got somebody to cover for me."

"You call out a lot. How does that work? Don't your supervisors get upset?"

"They don't care as long as somebody can take the shift."

"Yeah, but still, you clearly have bills to pay."

"This house is paid for. And besides, I now have a roomie, so a lot of my bills are cut in half." He sat back in his seat and put his hands behind his head. "This island life is sweet."

"Well, I rushed home because I wanted to tell you something. That guy that Mr. Clayton saw at the bung—"

"Ah!" Ali sprang back up and cut me off.

"There was somebody at ch—"

"Nope!"

"Ali, I think I saw the guy—"

"Stop."

He looked at his watch and clapped his hands in resolution.

"We got somewhere to be," he said, "and I'm not talking about any of that crazy stuff tonight."

"Yeah, but you should probably know about this."

"Can it wait a little while? Things have been pretty quiet since you got here. I think that whatever was going on is over now. I think that investigation in Philly really did scare that guy off."

His confidence gave me a sense of assurance.

"Well, where are we supposed to be?"

"We're going to this comedy club in Hamilton. There's a lot of good talent here on the island, you'd be surprised. They serve some of the best seafood in the parish, and it's right on the water."

"Oh that sounds exciting! Let me go change real quick."

"What you have on looks good."

"Okay, but just let me freshen up. I'll be right back."

When I came back out, Ali cut the lights off and opened the door for me. I waited for him to lock it. Then, while I was still staring up at the gorgeous sky, I saw a stunning platinum necklace with a brilliant diamond cross passing below my eyes and landing around my neck.

"Whoa! What is this for?" I asked.

"You'll be gone by the time your birthday comes. Anyway, a gift doesn't have to be 'for' something. I thought it would be perfect on you, and it is."

I thanked him and got a little flustered as he stood with his back against the door admiring me in the necklace.

"Okay, now what? Are you supposed to thank him again, give him a hug, a kiss?"

This wasn't like when he got me the job and I immediately flung my arms around him, or any other time that I came home from work and lightheartedly planted a kiss on his eager lips. There was intensity in his expression, and I remembered that all that proximity and affection had to eventually lead somewhere.

"Dammit, and it's Sunday, too. You just left church!"

I had been on a good, holy roll. But now, there was that look. It was beyond the shy, retreating eye glance that a guy gives when he's interested from afar but can't figure out a way to talk to a girl. It was way past that goofy, nervous grin that two people give to each other during their first few times out on a date. This was a look I couldn't even poke fun at. It was that inescapable, squinty-eyed smoldering look of desire that a man no longer even cares to hide because he knows you feel the same way.

I didn't know what to say, but I soon didn't have to say anything as he gripped my waist and pulled me into the kiss. If there was any doubt in his mind that I would accept his invitation, it melted away with the clasping of my hands behind his head. He tightened his grip on my waist and we held our embrace there, in the shadow of a setting sun.

It took a lot less time than I expected for me to completely lose myself in the moment. I never once stopped to consider the fact that I may be going a little too far, but only followed what seemed to be a natural flow. Before I knew it, I had spun around with my back against the door and Ali's hands were in my hair. I slipped one hand into his shirt and started unbuttoning it from the inside. My other hand had made its way down the arch of his back and came to rest on his backside.

"What are you doing?" he asked with a smirk.

"What? Whatever do you mean?"

"Uh, what was that?"

"What was what?" I asked, pretending to be coy and feeling impatient.

"Nothing… I just wasn't expecting that." he said with an expression on his face that was beginning to resemble discomfort. He rubbed his watch and looked nervously over his shoulder at his car then cleared his throat.

"The show starts soon, in like thirty, forty minutes. We should leave now to get good seats."

"Okay." I said.

I looked at him for a moment, trying to figure out why I'd made him so uneasy. Then we both got into the car.

Soon after we got on the main road, he took my hand gently but remained quiet. Then I saw him glance at me a few times out of the corner of my eye.

"What is the problem?!" I finally asked.

He chuckled and shook his head.

"What? You got a problem with a woman being expressive?"

"No." he said quietly. "I'm just surprised that you were." He scratched his head.

"Oh, I get it." I thought to myself.

"I mean, I'm standing there thinking, how long is this gonna go on before she starts to get a little shy. But hey, I mean, if it's not like I thought, that's cool. I'm not judging. I just thought it was something else. I was caught off guard, that's all."

"Well so was I." I said.

He started to speak again, paused then finally said,

"If I knew it was like that, I would have made my move a long time ago."

He started to chuckle but stopped when he turned to see my warning glare.

"I'm just playing!" he said.

He probably wasn't, but I let him off the hook.

He pulled into a parking space and we walked into the comedy club, leaving the awkwardness behind.

We enjoyed our dinner, remarkably without choking on the food after having laughed so much during the first two acts. At one point everything seemed so perfect that I began to regret that I wasn't what Ali originally thought I was.

He clearly had assumed I was a virgin, and if it hadn't been for Jack, I would be. But then, if it hadn't been for Jack, Ali and I would never have met.

As the third act entered the stage, Ali leaned in to tell me, "Oh, make sure you don't drink anything while this guy's up there. You will be on the floor laughing and choking!"

Everyone clapped to welcome him. I looked around the club to see the beautiful couples and jovial crowd around us and spotted a tall man by the bar. He was wearing a gray coat similar to the one worn by the man at church.

"Ali! Look at that guy over there."

"What?"

"The guy at the bar in the gray coat. Look."

"What about him?"

"He looks just like the guy Mr. Clayton described."

"No he doesn't. He doesn't look homeless."

"He looks like this guy I saw at church today. That's what I wanted to tell you. He came in, just stared at me during the ceremony, then left."

"Are you sure he looked just like that?"

"Well… he was about his height. The guy at church was dirtier, though."

"And I don't know too many homeless guys who wouldn't have already pawned a nice gold watch like that. There's more than one gray trench coat in Bermuda, Jane. Come on, just relax."

After the show, we got into the car exhausted from so much laughter. It was the perfect way to ease some of the tension caused by the guy in the trench coat and our fumbled intimate moment earlier that evening.

Before turning on the car, Ali turned toward me.

"There's something I been meaning to ask you, and it just came to my mind like a random thought for some reason. You said, when you were younger, you wanted to be an architect more than almost anything. What did you want more than that?"

I looked down at my right hand. For years following my parents' divorce, I had worn my mother's wedding ring on my right thumb. This was the ring that she'd purchased for herself so that she could appear to be the married woman she was. She had always described her love for my dad as a passion that no one else could ever understand. That ring was my reminder to avoid such passion like an STD. I never wanted to be so given over to love that I'd allow myself to be desperate or taken advantage of. The word love itself had become difficult to say.

For the first time I felt ashamed that I had been so adamant about avoiding love, like the ring thing might have been a bit of overkill. I covered my right hand as if the ring was still there, then I sat frozen hoping that Ali would simply forget that he'd asked me a question and drive off.

"Jane?"

"This. What we have. Or, what we might have. I don't know. That's what I wanted more than anything." I turned my head to look out the window and Ali started the car. We didn't say much during the ride home. We didn't need to.

21

"You have nice nails. You don't get 'em done?"

"Thanks. No. If I did, they wouldn't be nice for long. Those chemicals eat my nails up and make them brittle."

"The natural look is really nice on you."

"Well what I don't do in makeup and nails I make up for in clothes, shoes and hair."

"And personality."

"Awww. Why thank you, dear!"

"And poise."

"Stop it, you're too sweet."

"And sexiness."

"Oh, you noticed?" I said, hiding my face behind a hand of playing cards and pretending to be shy.

"You're quite a cultured and debonair fellow yourself. I've been checking out a few of your books— Francis Cress Welsing, Rushdie, Sacred Geometry. You know, brains are pretty darn sexy too."

"That accent of yours, it's interesting." he continued. "Your voice has a lower pitch, and with that slight drawl everything comes out sounding really relaxed and sultry. That is, if you ain't mad about something."

He paused to throw out one of the cards he held in hand.

"Like you about to be mad about this hand I got. Do you even know what you're doing over there?"

"No."

I gave up and put my cards on the floor.

"Poker is not my game, Ali. You might as well give up trying to teach me."

"Here, let's do this then." he said.

He opened up a new box of cards with the name *Instinct* on the front.

"You have to answer each question without thinking about it, like in two seconds. The idea is that your immediate answer is your most instinctive one, and therefore, your most honest. People like to play this game as an icebreaker, but it's good for getting into the heads of weirdos like you, too. Ready?"

"Yep." I smirked.

"Red or blue?"

"Blue."

"Night or day?"

"Night."

"Sesame Street or Fraggle Rock?"

"Fraggle Rock!"

"Hmmm, I knew it." he mused. "Bunch of underground weirdos. Chicken or shrimp."

"Shrimp."

"Fancy. Gospel or rap?"

"Gospel Rap."

"Straddling the fence, ay? Lust or Pride."

"What?" I asked, confused about the sudden jump from the mundane to the spiritually monumental.

"Hurry up and pick one."

"That's not in the cards!" I tried, unsuccessfully, to snatch the card from his hand then squinted my eyes in suspicion.

"Why would I pick either?" I asked in defiance.

"Just play the game."

"Lust. Okay my turn. Blind or deaf?"

"Mmm hmmm." he said. He must have thought lingering on my last answer would cause a segue into more intimate conversation. I widened my eyes to let him know that I was still waiting on his next response.

"Deaf." he finally said.

"Passion or practicality."

"Umm…"

"Come on, Ali, two seconds."

"But, wait a minute. That's a hard one. I mean, I guess I should choose practicality. But you gotta have some passion, right?"

"You are well over two seconds."

"Can I pass that one? I gotta think about it."

"Are you serious?!"

"Okay, okay. Practicality, I guess, but the jury's still out on that one, forreal."

"Land or sea?"

"Land."

"Adulthood or childhood?"

"See, that one… I'd go with childhood. I would love to be a kid again, ya know. But then, certain privileges come with adulthood. I would choose childhood, though, but just for a limited time."

"Cat or dog— I guess I know the answer to this."

"Dog." he said, nodding enthusiastically. "You're a cat person, aren't you?"

"Dogs are way too needy." I responded. "I admire the feline free spirit. Disability or death?"

"Mmm!" He looked at me as if there was a sudden stench in the air. "What's up with that?"

"What?"

"How you go from furry friends to maiming, mutilation and death?"

"Same way you went from music to the Seven Deadly Sins. It's the game. And it's not that serious, Ali. Death is a part of life. You can't have one without the other."

"See, I guess being really devout and all makes you more accepting to the idea of death. I guess I'm not afraid of death, I just don't want it to happen any time soon."

"Who does?"

"Oh, some people do. That's for sure."

"I don't get that." I said. "I mean, I can understand hard times, and being down and sometimes not seeing a way out. I just can't relate to the feeling of wanting to be permanently done with it all. The world is just too big— it offers the potential for so much more, even if you think you're finished. The closest I've ever come is just wanting to take a really long nap, like being in a coma."

This serious look came over his face, and he nodded slowly like he was beginning to understand something that had perplexed him before.

"A coma? You wished for a coma?"

"Sort of. I've never wanted to die. At my lowest points I just say to myself, if I could just get a break, just turn everything off and sleep for a month I'd be okay afterward. At least if I'm in a coma, when I come back I'd have a good excuse for missing class and work, and insurance would cover it."

That last part was meant to be a joke, but he missed it.

"So... that night on the rock— that night I met you—you weren't... on the verge of trying to induce a coma, were you?

"I knew it!" I said. "You thought I was crazy and suicidal."

He smiled and shook his head.

"Yeah, but then after you violated me I figured you were just drunk or high."

He went on, "There was this kid in my high school who killed himself senior year. I didn't really know him well, but I'd had a couple of classes with him and he seemed pretty normal. He was supposed to be going to an Ivy League school. People said it was the pressure and stuff at home. That was messed up. I never wanted to put that kind of pressure on myself. It's not worth it."

"I think some people romanticize death." I said. "They think it's gonna be some amazing supernatural experience. It's like the people who go ghost hunting, craving something out of the ordinary. Add the feeling that life has nothing more to offer and curiosity about a possible afterlife, and it's not hard to understand. I've never taken the romanticizing that far, but I have this thing about cemeteries."

"Really?" He asked.

"Yeah, there's this beautiful cemetery in Philly, my favorite, called Laurel Hill. It's huge. I can walk around for hours there. It really lives up to the name 'cement city' because the monuments are so detailed and architectural, so big. And it's so peaceful. You know, cemeteries are some of the most peaceful places on earth."

"I'll bet." Ali said sarcastically.

"Forget you! Anyway, the dead don't bother me. It's the living who are the problem. What were we talking about before all this?"

"You were gonna tell me about your first time."

"No, I wasn't."

"I'm pretty sure I asked that."

"Pretty sure you didn't."

"Checkers?"

"Cool."

We set up the board and, after our first few moves, Ali immediately started trying to move pieces backward in order to skip mine.

"Why are you such a cheat?" I said while yanking back one of my stones.

"This isn't cheating, this is strategy."

"It's a cheating strategy! There are rules to this game for a reason."

"Jane, don't you know rules are relative? They're made up. You gotta learn when to follow the rules and when they don't matter."

That sounded like something Jack would say.

"Oh really, Mr. I'm nervous because a girl put her hand on my butt!"

"Nervous? I wasn't nervous. I was trying to be respectful. And shoot, I'm not trying to get tied up with you. We haven't covered preliminaries." He smirked, "I'm still an American citizen, and I don't want anything to do with those child support laws. I'll be broke before I can figure out what I wanna do with my life."

"Fool, please!" I laughed and scanned the board deciding on my next move. "What would I want from you— this old house and your uncle's boat? Well, hold on, that could pay down some tuition."

"Uh huh. Talkin' about *Georgia O'Keefe* and all her flower innuendo. No telling what you could be into."

My eyes widened upon his assumption. He had lightened the mood by covering the subject with some humor, and even though I knew sex shouldn't be hard to talk about at this point, I hadn't expected to be answering questions about my history over a game of checkers.

"That's none of your business." I said, casually dismissing the topic.

"No, I think it might be my business."

"Oh, really?"

"Yeah, how does everything that's been going on here factor into your, uh, upholding biblical principles and all that, anyway?"

"Exactly what are you referring to, Ali?"

"This is your little game, acting all innocent. I saw your pills. So how many men have you been with?"

If he had asked in some other, less accusing way I might have been inclined to answer simply, but this just pissed me off.

"There are a few reasons a woman could be on birth control that have nothing to do with preventing pregnancy, Ali."

"Got that poor African boy all worked up and then just dumped him. He missed meals because of you."

He just barely redeemed himself with that little joke.

"Get outta here!" I laughed.

"What's the purpose of trying to hide it?"

"And what exactly is the purpose of this interrogation? You don't have to know where I've been. I don't have to answer to you for anything. Ain't like anything is about to pop off with YOU right now, anyway!"

"Yeah, okay. Not sure what to make of you." He gave me another one of those playfully suspicious winks.

"Well, if you don't know what to do with it, somebody else will." I grinned.

Game! I was sure that was the end of it and that I'd had the last word.

"I guess your feelings must still be all in a jumble about that guy back home. That must be the reason for your... vacillation."

"What vacillation? I went for it and you chumped down!"

"Yeah, but if you were really serious you would have taken it all the way."

Surely he was attempting to repair his own ego with that comment. He paused, apparently waiting for something to really get under my skin.

"You still dodging my question, but I think I pretty much got it figured out."

I just stared at him, kind of angry but unable to deny being curious about how he planned to wrap this up.

"I can understand. I mean, it's one thing to lose your virginity. It's a whole other thing to lose it to some obsessed old dude with stalky tendencies who thinks you're his property now because he was the one who—"

"Slow down, Sherlock." I interrupted. "You're sounding pretty stalky now, yourself. You think you got me all figured out?"

"It isn't that hard to figure out. Him snooping around on you across all this distance and you still trying to act like an innocent church girl while you're living here with me. You haven't been out of the yard for *that* long."

I stood up slowly and looked at him. I didn't want to shut him out, but somehow, I felt overexposed. He essentially belittled my attempt at renewed discipline as an "act" and made me feel like he really didn't understand where I was coming from. It was like he thought he had one up on me. Maye that was his point.

"What?" he asked, confused.

I started walking down the hall but stopped to give him one more disapproving look when he asked again,

"What? Where are you going."

"Do I need your permission to use the bathroom?" I snapped.

Actually, I went to my bedroom. I needed a breather. It had almost felt like we might be able to pick up where we left off before the comedy show. But with the way we were both fumbling that conversation, I had my doubts about how things might turn out in bed.

A few moments later, the phone rang. I could hear Ali answer it in the living room.

"Hello... Hello?"

He hung up.

It rang again.

"Hello? Ay, who is this?"

He hung up again.

The phone rang a third time. Ali picked up and didn't say anything, but folded his arms and squinted his eyes in a silent standoff with the caller. Then he hung up again.

A few moments later, I resurfaced in the living room having partially recovered from our conversation. We tried to settle back into our game and played for another few minutes.

Then there was a loud knock at the back door.

Ali got up slowly and walked cautiously through the kitchen to see who was there. I followed closely behind.

Just as Ali approached the door a shadowy figure ran past the window.

"Who the hell is *this*?" Ali whispered.

He went to the hallway closet and grabbed a handgun from the top shelf.

We huddled in his bedroom near a window which faced the direction the figure ran in. There was banging on a window in the living room and a crash.

Then we heard someone speak.

"Alright, young bucks, that's enough playin' house!"

I felt my body go limp for a split second at the sound of his voice. It was searing, and so immediate and familiar, as if it had never been absent. It inspired so much fear.

We waited for him say or do something else.

"You might as well come on out!" Jack said. "Easy way or the hard way? What y'all want?"

There was silence for who knows how long then the sound of aggressive footsteps coming in our direction.

"It took a long time for me to get here, Jane, and I ain't tryna be here all night!"

At that moment, Ali had enough. It had appeared as though he was staying close to me in order to keep me safe or make me feel safe. But he clearly thought it was time to stand up and do something.

"Goddammit!" he said as he stood up and pushed away my hand which I had extended to try and stop him.

He opened the door fast, slamming it against the wall. Jack turned around and looked at him as if to say, *"Well it's about damn time."*

"That's enough of these scare tactics and *bullshit*. What is this? What do you think you're doing in my house?"

"No brotha, what are you doing? That's the question," Jack said calmly with his arms folded. "What *you* been doing? I asked you to take care of this situation for me. What the hell you been up to?"

I looked at Ali while he continued to stare Jack down holding the gun.

"Yeah, you done had a nice lil' vacation with my money." Jack said. "Been having dinner with my money, going to shows with my money, paying ya bills with my money. Even that platinum necklace around her throat—MY damn money!"

"Ali, what is he talking about?" I asked.

I wanted to put up a united front in this situation, but the idea that he had been in cahoots with Jack all this time was far too overwhelming. He gave me a tentative glance, but kept the gun focused on Jack.

"I swear, girl," Jack went on, "you bout the most indecisive lil' chick I ever seen! First you wanna work for me then you don't. You in school then you ain't. You wanna be my lady, then you skip town."

He looked at Ali with a sly grin.

"She took every bit o' that money, though. She didn't have to think long and hard about that. And one thing I know for sure. As wonderful a guy as you may think you are, my brotha, I know she won't givin' it up for nothing!"

Ali clutched the gun that much harder.

"Jack! What do you think this is going to accomplish?" I asked, exhausted and just wanting something to propel this nightmare toward its end.

"I know you wanted me to keep my promise, Jane." he said, almost with a hint of compassion. "That's what I'm trying to do. That's all I'm trying to do."

Jack reached around his waist and in a flash, Ali pulled the trigger. The bullet just missed Jack and instead hit the lamp next to where he was standing. Jack ran and jumped back out of the window. Ali ran behind him.

"Where are you going?" I yelled.

"Just stay here!"

I grabbed the phone to call the police, but there was no dial tone. When I ran to my room to get my cell phone, I heard two more gunshots ring out.

"Hello, yes. There was just a break-in at our home! My boyfriend chased the guy out of the house, and I just heard gunshots!"

"Where are you located, ma'am."

"We're at 11 Saltwater Lane, just across from the Jobson's Cove Haven resort. They were running in the direction of that resort."

"Ma'am, do you recall what the intruder was wearing?"

"H-he had on all black, a tailored suit with shirt and tie. Ali, my boyfriend, had on gray sports pants and a red t-shirt."

"Ali? This address sounds familiar. Is this Alister Stevens you're referring to? My family was good friends with his uncle. Used to always see him at the music festivals."

"Yes! Yes!"

"I'm sorry, Ma'am. We're sending someone right out. Please stay inside. The police will be there shortly."

I turned out the remaining lights and hid in my bedroom closet. There was no more noise from outside, and I listened for the sound of sirens for what felt like an eternity.

Next, I faintly heard a key being inserted into the back door, and then it opening. His footsteps didn't have a consistent rhythm, making me think that Ali had been hurt and was limping as a result of the exchange. As he got closer to the bedroom door, I got out of the closet and hurried to open it.

It took one solid blow from Jack's fist to send me flying backward and onto a trunk where I bumped my head. I lay there fading as a peculiar and emotional Jack held my head and started talking.

"Why is this happening? It wasn't supposed to be like this, Jane. This wasn't what I wanted. I loved you. I showed you I loved you. I watched over you… all this time. Everything you needed, *everything,* I gave you that. Now I'm 'sposed to chase yo' ass halfway round the world or wait for you to make up your mind 'bout what you gon' do? I can't be spendin' up my resources, sendin' guys here and there just to keep you in check and then you get 'em all distracted. This is quality time that we coulda had together. I told you I would keep my promise to you—well I had a promise to keep to myself, too."

I floated in and out of consciousness, but he kept a tight grip on my chin and shook it whenever I was about to fade out.

"You don't understand. You don't understand what love is. You're just a pretty little mess— you have no idea what love is! But that's alright. You don't have to worry about makin' any more hard choices. I got you now."

***

I came to in the back of a rented Mercedes with a gag around my mouth and several twist ties binding my wrists.

I knew Jack was attempting to high tail it off the island, and I had no idea where he was planning to end up. I overheard the tail end of a conversation he had with someone who was waiting on one of the smaller islands with a private plane.

I figured he must have had several people in Bermuda working along with his plan— Ali, the guy in the trench coat, and who knows who else. It dawned on me that he had to be much more than a real estate investor.

He had removed his jacket and tie and was calmly chatting as if he was ordering pizza.

I thought of my mother back home who was probably sleeping in her bed that very moment with no idea of the danger I was in. Worse yet, what if she could sense I was in danger and couldn't do a thing about it? I thought about my brother, knowing that he would throw everything he had into consoling my mother after such a tragedy. Who would take care of him? And my dad? I'd never have the chance to see him age, mature, and get better. I'd never have the chance to know him well and have something that felt like a true relationship with him.

Even if Jack had initially enlisted Ali to keep me in check, it was obvious that he wasn't on Jack's side. The worst thoughts about what might have happened to Ali started creeping into my mind, and I stopped them right away. I couldn't sit back and let all this happen without a fight. I remembered the fearless lioness from that dream I'd had at the beginning of my trip. Jack was no true ringmaster. I knew that lioness was alive within me, and, if necessary she would die fighting to live.

I slowly pushed my torso forward and off of the seat. I couldn't remove the gag, but I knew my front teeth were the sharpest ones in my mouth, and the gag had left them exposed.

At one point, as Jack pulled out of Ali's driveway, he accidentally dropped his phone, and a left turn sent it tumbling onto the passenger side floor. He stopped the car and leaned over to get it. As he rose back up, I pushed my body forward with all the upper body strength I could muster and sank my teeth into the side of his neck, determined to remove a chunk of skin.

He latched onto my head to pry me off but screamed helplessly upon sensing the first bit of tearing flesh. He tried to strike me, and I knew that I'd have to release him in order avoid another blackout. I pushed myself backward onto the seat. As he turned around to seize me, his face instead met the bottoms of my sneakers and he went flying back onto the dashboard.

He sat stunned with blood pouring from his nose. His grip on my head and the subsequent commotion had loosened the blood-soaked gag, which slipped off my mouth and onto the floor.

"Bitch, you think you so smart," he said, full of fatigue and frustration and trying to catch his breath.

With adrenaline like I'd never felt before fueling me, I screamed at the top of my lungs then started bouncing up and down on the seat, rocking the car back and forth, thrashing against the seats. My hair was flying, I was growling and snapping my teeth as Jack tried to grab me again.

"Girl, you better not tear up this damn car!"

I kept screaming and Jack moved forward, attempting to dodge my feet in order to get a hold of me.

"Stop it! Calm yo' ass down!"

He squared up to hit me several times but hesitated.

"I'm tryin' not to hit you again, dammit, calm down!"

I hauled off and spit in his face. He grabbed my neck and stared me down. Neither of us changed our expression until my body began to go limp and he released my neck.

He left me in the back seat, opened his door and stepped out to make another call.

"Man, you gotta meet me at another spot, somewhere closer. This girl bout to lose her mind… There's a private dock about a hundred yards from the resort… Look, you the one let her get on the plane in the first place— don't fuck this up, too! Just do it… alright."

I noticed that the back seat cigarette lighter had been depressed during my fit, and I hunched down to grab it between my teeth.

He opened my door and pulled me out of the car with his arms around my chest. When we were standing up straight, I jumped several times and landed at least once on his foot. When I bent down and burned his hand with the cigarette lighter, he instinctively let me go, and I ran around to the other side of the car.

After I screamed a few times and tripped on the gravel, Jack nabbed me again and started dragging me toward the small, private dock. From the dock I could see police gathering on the street in front of the resort and I began screaming at them.

"HEEEEEELP! OVER HEEEEEEEEERE!"

I broke away again and ran back and forth from one side of the dock to the other, lunging and kicking at Jack in order to avoid being caught. I could see that he was limping from when I stomped on his foot, and one sudden move to grab me twisted his ankle and sent him plunging into the bay. I made off down the short boardwalk and saw Ali break through the trees that shrouded the dock.

"Ali! He fell in the water!"

We went running and soon Jack emerged from the bay, still limping. He ran across the sand after us. Soon the only place to hide was in the shadows of the huge limestone rocks that dotted the shoreline.

Ali grabbed the gun from his hip. I frantically scraped the twist ties across the rock in order break them. Finally, they popped and I was free. I threw my arms around Ali and squeezed.

"I thought Jack shot you."

"It only grazed my arm, but I got his gun."

I looked at the wound on Ali's right forearm and covered my mouth in shock.

We heard a sudden splash of water and looked around. Jack stuck his head out from behind one of the smaller rocks that he had started climbing.

"Shoot him!" I yelled.

"These rocks are too close. I need a better shot, or the bullet could ricochet and hit one of us."

"It's jagged limestone! What are you worried about? Shoot him!"

Before Ali could pull the trigger, Jack leaped off the rock and onto him. They wrestled for control of the gun. Entangled in one another's grip, they fell into the water and scrambled back up again.

As they tussled, I remembered a pile of small rocks that sat along the steps of the rock formation that I often rested on at the beginning of my trip. Without thinking I ran up the steps to get them.

Jack immediately jumped up to pursue me. I raised a rock to throw it at him but saw Ali not far behind him, and I didn't want to risk causing Jack to fall back onto him. Though Ali had reclaimed his gun from the water, shooting at a moving target in the dark with me standing nearby proved a challenge. When they reached the top, there was nowhere for any of us to go.

Jack grabbed my hair and turned to face Ali.

"What you wanna do, man? You don't know what you doin'. If you had any kinda aim, you would've shot me by now… You wanna try to shoot me up here and risk this girl catching a bullet? Be sensible."

Ali stepped slowly closer as Jack moved toward the edge of the rock, pulling me with him. Jack sighed as if extremely annoyed.

"I don't believe this… Y'all just don't know when to quit."

He released my hair and pushed me in Ali's direction.

They stood face to face, each honing in on a weakness in the other. Jack lunged for Ali's arm and twisted it behind his back. Ali broke away and landed two punches in Jack's face. Jack went to rush Ali and they both landed on the ground with Jack hovering over the younger man. Jack put his hands around Ali's neck, but Ali head butted him in the face and knocked him onto his back.

When Jack looked up and saw that Ali was nearly standing, he tried to get up just as quickly. Instead, he rolled over and ended up too close to the edge where loose stones began to shift and roll off the rock formation. He stopped for a second with one leg dangling off the cliff. Then he reached for a protruding rock in front of him and tried to pull himself up.

I could see the rock wobbling tentatively, attempting to give way, seemingly wanting to do something to end it all, but still unsure. There was no more room for indecision.

I stepped forward quickly and gave the rock a firm kick. It gave way, and Jack went sliding over the edge. He bounced off the cliff face once then finally came to rest on the coral just beneath the water. He was rendered immobile by the fall, and twitched for several seconds as bubbles drifted to the water's surface. Then the bubbles stopped.

***

"Is he dead? *God,* please tell me his ass is dead."

I grabbed Ali's shoulder and leaned forward to look over the cliff edge again. The water at the foot of the limestone rock was shallow and pristine and swayed gently against the black on black suit which fit the body beneath it to a T. Jack's tawny skin shined in the moonlight, as radiant as ever. It looked like he had unknowingly dressed for his own funeral.

Ali, breaking from the shock, turned slowly toward me and stared like he couldn't remember where he was or who I was.

"Language?" he asked.

"What?" I asked, confused and a little pissed that he was choosing to judge me *now.*

"You cussin' now?"

I had just facilitated the death of a human being and he was concerned about my use of a bad word.

"Was that supposed to be a prayer?" Ali pressed me for an explanation as if this was some moment of truth in which I had to redeem my good name, or else.

I snapped back, "Would you prefer that it not be answered? Do you remember what happened tonight?"

Sirens grew ever louder, filled the silence between us, and finally drowned out the sound of the waves which had given me so much peace just a few hours before. Red and blue flashes swallowed up the moonlight and bounced against the rock's jagged edges. Ali took my hand and slowly helped me down by way of the sturdy steps carved into the rock's side, just the way he had in the beginning.

The touch of his hand was calming. Without him saying a word I felt that he had already forgiven me and that, as always, he saw me and still loved me.

22

Just before I was released from the hospital, investigators arrived and pressed me for any additional information about Jack. They never once questioned our story on how he died.

"He kidnapped me. He chased us. They were fighting. He slipped and fell off the cliff and into the bay."

They had already caught on to the fact that Jack was a shady character after doing a little digging around with the Philly police.

"He's dead." I argued with the officers. "Why does anything about him matter now? I've already answered enough questions!"

"Miss, in order to be sure that no further danger exists, we have to know whether or not he came here alone.

Didn't you say he was on the phone with someone when he kidnapped you?"

"Yeah, but I doubt he would have any interest in me independent of Jack. He was just the guy with the plane."

"Was there anything else about Jack, anything he said, or did, something about his work, that we haven't discussed? Did you know any of his associates?"

"No."

I didn't want to talk about him anymore. I had accomplished a lifetime of pious chastity, crying rivers at the altar whenever I so much as lusted in my heart, or enjoyed those intimate moments of self-discovery. I turned my nose up at countless guys because they weren't Christian, because they were unworthy, too much of a distraction. All that self-restraint, that lofty commitment to remain excellent and pure, had gone down the drain when I let my guard down and fell for the guy who I thought understood and believed in me. Now I had to deal with this. I didn't know how much of this thing with Jack had been real or how much of it was contrived. And now he was dead.

***

Two days later, we received a call from another investigator, asking us to come into the station. When we arrived, neither of us could read her expression.

"I wanted you here in person so we could tell you all that we learned about Jack and help to put your mind at ease. We contacted Philadelphia police and they shared some of their findings with us. First of all, there doesn't appear to be anyone else involved in the stalking. In a way, you really dodged a bullet. These traffickers are extremely clever. But they usually aren't this persistent with young women with roots like yourself."

"I'm sorry, did you say *traffickers*?" I almost lost my voice on that last word.

The investigator breathed and continued slowly with an empathetic tone.

"He apparently has a connection to someone— possibly a relative— who is involved in trafficking young women around the United States. It looks like that was who spotted you first. Jack was supposed to vet you on that person's behalf, but it appears as though he developed an unusual interest in you and wanted you for himself.

"Now, based on some of the information shared with us, this guy has been following you for quite a bit of time. He's originally from Portsmouth, Virginia, and he moved to Philadelphia in January 2003. He's a real estate investor and hard money lender. He wasn't the most scrupulous of financiers, apparently, and there's a trail of developing evidence which suggests that a few people got hurt in connection with that."

"He's from Portsmouth, *twenty minutes* away from my home town?" I asked. "2003's the same year I moved to Philly."

I felt the intensity of my emotions ratcheting up.

"Ma'am, this man has been obsessed with every move you've made for the last four years. Authorities searched his home and found hundreds of pictures and journals documenting his obsession with you.

"One video in particular, recorded on September 19, 2002, was taken by Jack to document the first day he ever talked to you. He must have been wearing a camera.

"You're not the first woman he's been violent with. He has a long history of domestic violence, and the testimonies of both his ex-wives show that. His first wife's brother shot him and his second wife ran him over while trying to get away from him during a fight. I guess he's had a few brushes with death prior to."

"Third time's a charm." Ali said.

"What about the video of the first time I talked to him?" I said abruptly. "I wanna see it. Can I see it?"

The surprised investigator looked at Ali as if she hoped he would jump in and stop me.

"Are you sure you want to do that? Jane, the fact that Jack is dead and that all this is over without either of you being seriously hurt is *good* news."

She was trying to turn on her big sister tone with me. I appreciated her caring way, I really did, but I had to know more.

She went on, "Situations like this rarely turn out this way. The ability to leave this all behind should give you great solace."

"I wanna see the video."

She began accessing the file on her computer.

We were at my church in Norfolk. It was the church I'd been a member of since committing to my faith several years before, a progressive, nondenominational megachurch with five thousand members and television cameras perched on the columns that supported the overflow seating. Praise and worship had just ended with uproarious shouting and clapping while someone approached the podium for announcements.

There I was. I was chatting quietly with my friends Katrina, Patricia and Joi. We were preparing to give our offerings.

"Here, miss." a man was saying to me.

I watched myself turn around to face the person tapping me on the shoulder. I suddenly remembered the first time I ever saw Jack's sharp, square-ish face and those thick curved brows. There hadn't been a hint of guile in his expression. He was handing me something.

"I think this is your license. It must have fallen out of your purse."

"Oh, thank you so much. Don't wanna lose that!" I said.

"Nice name."

"Thanks."

After the clip ended, I didn't budge. I waited to see more, but the investigator said, "So why don't you two head back home and—"

"How long are you gonna do this?" Ali asked. "You're never gonna figure this out. Crazy doesn't have any rhyme or reason that you would understand. We need to leave."

He stood up and extended his hand to help me up. I thanked the officer sincerely for her help.

Ali mumbled, "I'll be damned if I'm gonna to sit here and watch this crazy ass fool on my time off."

He shook the investigators hand. "Thank you for everything. I really appreciate you explaining this for us."

As we rode back home, I wanted to feel comforted by the fact that Jack was dead. But knowledge of his activities had only heightened my awareness of just how close danger could be at any moment. The world was full of Jacks, and I was convinced there was something in particular about me that was attracting them.

"How you feeling?" Ali asked. He was doing what he could to help me calm down. For the first time, I realized that there was also something very promising within me that made it possible for me to connect with him. As keen as I had been on attracting mishap, I was just as capable of attracting something incredibly good.

***

"I've decided to go back home early, Ali. My family will want to be near me and see that I'm okay. I'll spend a good amount of time with them and then do a few things to get ready for the fall semester."

Ali kept looking ahead as he steered his uncle's boat along the bay. He nodded but said nothing.

"But I want to come back, maybe even spend the summer here. This place has become a second home to me and I want us to spend as much time together as possible. I know long distance can be tough, but we can both travel. And there are so many ways to keep in touch nowadays."

Ali looked troubled, and I could see that he was not sharing my enthusiasm. I caught myself being giddy and presumptuous and thought better of showing too much excitement.

"Ali, what is it? What do you think?"

He looked downward then back at the water.

"Hey, if the living situation makes you uncomfortable, I understand. I'm sure I can find somewhere else. I'll just get an early jump on one of the boarding houses and—"

"That's not a problem. It's not that." Ali said.

He blew out a heavy sigh.

"Then what is it?"

I tried to find my words but everything was starting to jumble in my head.

"Jane… I need to explain something to you… about what Jack said when he was in the house."

I waited quietly.

"A few hours before you checked into your bungalow, somebody called the front desk at the resort and asked for security. He made it sound like he was somebody from school, like something bad happened before you left and he just wanted to make sure you were okay. He asked me to kind of keep an eye on you and said he would check back with me periodically during your trip. He made you sound almost nutty, like you should have been on meds or had a chaperone or something. I had no idea that he was planning to come here, but after I met you, I just didn't feel right telling him your business like that."

I wasn't the least bit surprised. I didn't think anything could have surprised me at that point.

"When he called and I picked up the phone that night at your place, he was mad that I was there with you, but I played it off so you wouldn't get upset with me."

I nodded slowly.

"I don't know, Jane..." he went on. "Sometimes, I feel... like I've already played my role with you."

"What are you talking about?"

"You know, it's like the purpose for me meeting you, maybe... it's been served. Now that all the craziness is over, I... I don't want to be one other thing to get in your way. You're gonna finish school, and have an awesome career, and a great life. And well, I got a lot of loose ends to tie up."

He turned quickly toward me and said, "You have no idea how much I've gained just from knowing you. I really admire your discipline and your ability to keep trying. But I don't want to hold you back. And you seem okay for now, but this situation was really a lot for both of us."

I took in what Ali said and refused to feel the sting. Somewhere deep down, I had always expected this to end abruptly, sorely, not on my terms.

I couldn't cling to my expectations and demand that he change his mind, as much as I wanted to. Plus, I only would have made a fool of myself if I tried, and that certainly was not going to happen. He'd told me what he wanted and I had to respect the reality of the situation. The inner receptionist was back to work, and she reminded me to stay cool and positive and to appreciate all the good that had accompanied my stay with Ali.

"Well, everything happens for a reason." I said with a smile.

"But hey, I'm definitely up for a visit. My family's in Maryland and Philly's not too far away, right?"

It was obvious that we both wanted to quickly move on from what could have been a heartbreaking and pathetic moment. We started planning his visit to Philadelphia, naming all the events and attractions we might want to check out.

***

My last day in Bermuda was as wonderful as ever. We visited the Crystal Caves for a much more professional, safe, and illuminated (if not so romantic) tour. We took one more walk around Historic St George. Then we had dinner and went back to the beach where we first met.

It was another gorgeous, moonlit night, and I noted that the horrific events that happened there had not at all diminished the beauty of the place. We sat in each other's arms joking around, talking about all the things we had done, and about the future, until the sun appeared again.

After the airport attendant announced that it was time to board my flight, I let everyone go ahead of me in line so we could say one last goodbye. Our kiss was like it had always been, loving and sincere. I waved to Ali as I boarded the plane and felt a prompt shift in my demeanor as the door closed behind me.

The flight crew wrapped up their introduction and I ordered a glass of red wine. I put on my headphones and cranked up the volume after landing on a station that was playing *Just Gotta Make It* by Trey Songz and Twista.

When the song went off and we emerged over the water I allowed myself one short cry. I could feel it welling up into a knot in my throat and figured now would be the best time to release it. I would have one good, quiet cry and leave it here. I would let it hover in the clouds and dissipate in the wind. It was over.

23

Back home at my apartment in Philly, I felt refreshed and ready to face the realities of my world. I was ready to get back to work. Ali and I had talked several days a week while I visited my family in Virginia. We were still keeping in touch, excitedly planning our anticipated visit, but never actually setting a date in stone.

One day, a letter from him arrived in the mail. He had attached a picture of us at Beluga. I carefully placed it in the scrapbook that I had dedicated to memories from the trip.

Sitting down, I read the letter.

> *"I can't believe the winter came and went that fast. Seems like it was just yesterday that you were sitting on that rock talking to yourself..."*

"I was PRAYING!" I yelled at the letter then smiled.

"Oh, my bad. You were probably praying. I thought you were drunk at first, though! I thought I was going to have to get my friend to airlift you off that thing with his helicopter. But, thankfully, you were okay.

"I hope you don't feel uncomfortable with how fast things progressed between us. Just didn't seem like there was any point in wasting time. Maybe it's good that you decided to leave when you did, though— I might not have been able to handle you leaving if you'd stayed longer.

"I miss having you around. Now I can't sit back and wait for you to eat some shampoo I snuck into your yogurt cup!

"I'm sorry about that. OK, not really, that ish was funny! But for real, meeting you was one of the best things that could have happened to me, especially at that time. I'm a different person, and I can't believe such an amazing thing could come and go so fast. I nearly had to die because of you, but I promise I won't hold that against you… I can kinda see why you made dude so crazy.

"Meeting you made me realize that I've got a lot of work to do on myself. I don't know if you understand that, but I hope you will soon. Despite your little attitude, I could see that you were very special even when we first met.

"I'll never forget you. Even if there's always hundreds of miles between us, or if love comes again tomorrow and sends us in opposite directions, you'll always have a special place in my heart.

Ali"

"Excuse me?" I shook my head in disbelief. "Excuse me?"

I picked up the phone and called my girl, Katrina.

"Girl, does this sound like a goodbye to you?"

I read the letter to her and asked again,

"Does that sound like goodbye, a permanent *'goodbye, buzz the hell off, I'm trying to let you down gently because I never wanna see or speak to you again,'* BYE?"

"Hmph." was all Katrina could say.

"Can you believe that? Another one bites the dust! What does this make, number twenty, twenty-four, thirty?"

"Jane, you've only had one boyfriend before this."

"I'm not talking about boyfriends! I'm talking about all the guys, all this riff raff, all this non-serious, not ready for a real relationship with me B.S. that I can't seem to escape. I am sick of being the girl who guys admire but who only the crazy ones want to hold on to."

"Girl, maybe you should call him to find out more. Maybe his head is messed up from what happened. Just call him."

"No. And what is this mess about *'even if love comes again tomorrow and sends us in opposite directions'*— what is that?"

"I don't know, girl."

"I mean *'tomorrow'* is pretty damn specific. What the heck is he talking about?"

"Sound like another woman to me."

"Uh huh. He's made his choice, and I don't chase anybody when they make it clear that they don't want to be bothered."

Katrina sighed. "Then it's done."

"Damn right, it's done."

And that was it. I burned the letter at the stove and permanently ended it, just the way Ali would have wanted it. I didn't hear from or call him again.

***

"You torched the boy's letter?" Devi asked.

"I couldn't have it lying around. I needed to."

"For what?"

"For closure. With Jack, my closure was knowing he was dead. This is like that."

"So Ali's dead to you?"

"No, not dead. Just done."

"I sure hope you don't change your mind when you're sixty and want to take a walk down memory lane."

"I'm not wishing the man any ill will, Devi. I'm just trying to get past it."

"What did you learn?"

"Here she goes again," I thought. I put my anger on pause and took a deep breath. I really did want to get this right.

"I guess my greatest take away was the realization of what love can be, what it's supposed to look like for me. I learned that I can be happy with a guy, that it's possible. I learned that I can have a guy in my life who isn't gay or only wanting to hop in bed, and we can have a lot of fun together. Good guys do exist. When my guard is down, and I'm not expecting the worst, I can let in a more positive experience. And I guess I at least have to respect him for being honest."

Devi affirmed my observations and then spoke her mind.

"We must learn to detach from outcomes. Stop the expectations. Stop all the holding on to what doesn't belong to us. None of it belongs to us, even when it claims to." She gave me a moment of silence to ponder her words, then continued.

"The good that you experienced is the most important thing to remember here. Don't throw the baby out with the bath water. It's okay to keep the good memories. You'll forget about Ali, the person, sooner than you think. It's the lesson that counts."

"You know, I had that dream again."

"The one with your grandmother at the barbecue?"

"Yeah. I had it a few times in Bermuda. I had it again last night. I've never had it this many times in such a short period."

"Could you understand anything that she said?

"Not the part I always hope to understand. But you know what I think? I think God is trying to show me that she's passing the baton to me. My Grandma Sadie's life was so full of struggles that I should learn from. Maybe that's what the dreams are about.

"I think this generational curse that seems to hover over women in my family, all these having ups and downs with men, is supposed to stop with me. I have to do something different! I mean, my mom was in an abusive marriage. Both my grandmothers were in abusive marriages. Seems like half my aunts took the same path at some point, and my grandma Sadie dated a married man for thirty years! That's not going to be my destiny. At convocation last year, the visiting Bishop declared us curse breakers, and that's what I'm gonna be!"

"Okay," Devi pleaded, "can you stop for a minute?"

"It's a new day! I know, with God's power, I can do this. I can find and hold on to real love. I'm not going to compromise. I'm not going to sit around and let some man abuse me. I'm not going to let my children grow up watching me waste away in a bad situation!"

"Are you going to stop talking?" Devi asked again.

"What?!"

"Stop for a minute. Whenever we have one of these talks, you go on and on about generational curses this and the devil that. What curse?! Jane, you are not cursed! And it is not your job to pick up where the women before you left off. This ain't a relay race!"

"You can only live *your* life, Jane. Forget about curses and boogeymen and running around with an 'S' on your chest. Just live your life. The women in your family experienced difficult circumstances and hardships; they had to make choices that you couldn't begin to understand. Stop judging them! You're young. You have time to make plenty of mistakes and learn your own lessons. And trust me, you will! Please, take the overwhelming responsibility of being some hero off your shoulders."

I was stunned by Devi's response. It was so different from the things I had been taught over the years. At church, it was drilled into us that we were curse-breakers, world-changers, the few chosen and enlightened youth who would take the planet by storm and win victory after victory for Christ. For the first time, I started to see just how arrogant that assumption was, and it was nice to have someone lift that load. I was speechless.

"Jane," she asked, "are you still there?"

"Yeah, umm… well I think you make some valid points."

"What did your grandmother say to you in the dream, the part you could understand?"

I shook myself out of shock in order to remember the dream's ending.

"Okay, the dream started like it always does, at the barbecue with all the kids playing and people walking around eating. Except… oh yeah, this time it was near dark. Grandma looked like she did just before she passed, thinner, hunched over in her chair, she was a little confused about where she was. But when she saw me, she lit up. Her eyes sparkled and she smiled that broad, cheeky smile. Her dark skin looked healthy and radiant, shiny, even though there was little light outside."

"I made small talk with my aunts as we stood around her, and she just stared at me with this look, like she was so happy and at peace. She reached in her pocket for that thing again, that plant. It was a tiny four-leaf clover with the roots dangling at the bottom. I leaned in as close as I could, and she said that thing that I can never understand.

"She called my name, and I said '*What, Grandma Sadie?*' She called me again, like I hadn't even responded. I was patient, figuring it was the confusion. Then she called me again.

"Finally, as I was saying something to one of my aunts, she grabbed my shoulders and just yelled at me, '*Listen to me, Jane!*' I was confused, because I had been listening, I just couldn't understand. She screamed, '*Listen… Listen!*' Then I woke up."

The memory of that ending to the dream unnerved me even in the telling of it.

"Jane, don't you get it? It's simple." Devi said.

I was clueless and frustrated by the fact that Devi seemed able to figure this out so quickly when this dream had perplexed me for years.

"Your very name is Luck." she continued. "I know you don't *believe* in luck, per se, but, if you can appreciate the metaphor, just listen. This is what we've been working toward all along, but now your subconscious mind is making the connection."

"Okay." I said in anticipation.

"Obviously the four-leaf clover is a symbol of luck. But it's a plant with the roots still attached. The opportunity exists for you to plant, to cultivate that four-leaf clover into something that will grow and multiply. You see, it's about creating your own destiny. But you have to listen to the lessons that life gives you and take *control* of your own life. What's controlling it right now?"

"I guess that kind of makes sense," I said. "But… it all sounds kind of… unspiritual, likes it's me in control of my life and not God. I dunno."

"*You* don't know about a lot of things." she sighed. "Why don't you just pray that whatever important message the dream has for you will become clear in due time?"

"That sounds reasonable." I said.

"Good."

24

I got ready for class after an energizing breakfast, a workout, and devotion. Knowing that such a fruitful morning would soon turn into a hectic workday, I savored every minute.

I decided to take the bus to school since I had an interview for an internship later that day, and I didn't want to battle for a parking space in Center City at lunch time.

After getting off the bus, I saw a familiar car pulling up next to me. The burgundy Honda Accord belonged to a guy I met at class registration, an MBA student from Liberia. He'd asked for my number and I had declined. He gave me his instead and I never called him. I had found him to be short, and not particularly attractive.

"Miss Jane. Hope you're having a good start to the year."

"And you as well, Issa."

"You know, I waited for your call and never heard from you. I figured you were much too busy getting ready for classes. You architects don't have time for much besides the studio."

I nodded and grinned.

"You have to eat some time, right? Maybe I can join you for lunch?" he insisted.

I could have simply said I wasn't interested, but that would have been a lie. His persistence was intriguing, and I didn't want to totally judge a book by its cover or write him off without even one real conversation.

"I have an appointment at lunch time." I said. "But dinner might work."

From The Author

Joy Outlaw
www.inanna-joy.com

I'm an inspirational author who uses snippets from my journey of life and love—my questions, problems, screw-ups, and victories, and those of the people around me—to fuel self-discovery. I'm a curious observer and determined seeker, sharing my lessons and not-so-humble opinions with anyone who'll delight in pondering with me.

Georgia-born and Virginia-bred, I'm currently making a life in the mid-atlantic U.S. region with two fascinating tweens who call me "mom". I'm a writer for hire with a slew of creative endeavors and career attempts in my wake. Somewhere along the way, I picked up some descriptors: Mystic Muse, Scribbling Sphinx, Wondering Woman, Nightshift Novelist… The evolution is real and it continues daily.

Words are my stock and trade and the primary medium with which I paint my destiny. I believe that everything begins with them. They are the spells we use to destroy and create. I enjoy creating most, and I intend to make some pretty good shit. So strap in. It'll be a bumpy ride, and it'll only get better.

Wait! Don't leave yet.

We've only just begun.

Thanks for reading Pretty Little Mess. Are you ready to grab,

Things Fall Together,

also part of the Jane Luck Adventures series? Awesome! While you're visiting amazon.com/author/joyoutlaw, please leave a review. Your thoughts in the conversation will invite others to discover this dynamic series and the alluring author behind this and many other captivating stories.

Share your thoughts now and stay tuned for more!

Made in the USA
Middletown, DE
15 June 2024

55846299R00172